Great
Gatsby
Revisited

A.D. Padgett

Published by
The Auditors of God

First Published 2012
Copyright Anthony Padgett 2012

ISBN 978-0-9572919-0-4

Great Gatsby Revisited

A.D. Padgett
(M.A., P.G.C.E., B.A.)

Of all that lovely, of all those brief
Hopes that went bravely beyond belief,
Of life's deep blazon with love's gold stain
Passing all reason doth aught remain?

ENVOI – HUMBERT WOLFE

Dedicated to STS.

Chapter 1

IT WAS THE summer of 2012, the year of the Dragon. A time of the Queen's Diamond Jubilee and the Olympic Games in London. But something much more memorable happened in my life that year. And I need to tell the tale, I can't keep it to myself any longer. You may have heard of the Great Gatsby, a character in a book written 90 years ago by F. Scott Fitzgerald. A character in a tale of decadence and love. Well I want to write about a real Great Gatsby.

I think it was Confucius who said, "a wise man criticises himself, a fool criticises others." So I leave it up to you, dear reader, to be the judge of him, myself and, in the end, of yourself as well.

I had always wanted to be a writer or a painter, but despite my lineage, being a relative of the 1920's poet Humbert Wolfe, I had never managed to get any work published or prestigiously exhibited. I scraped a disreputable 2:2 in English Literature at Oxford University, so I never thought it wise to become a writer. And my daubs on canvas never got any further than local art society walls though I was frequently told by all who knew me that I had a great talent.

Despite partying and living in a noisy room at the entrance of Trinity Quad my years at Oxford had left me addicted to the dependability of convention, fostered by such a safe and timeless place. So I moved into a life of respectability and my relatives were able to arrange a comfortable job for me in credit and investment securities. And there I remained, until the axe fell.

I made a little money selling bonds in London, so when I lost my job in the banking crisis it was an opportunity to move away from the drudge, from the lugubrious daily grind of the City. I had some savings and Zhang Xing, the husband of Rose Goldsmith, my second cousin once removed, owned some lodges in the more salubrious Lake District in the North West of

England. And the rent was cheap enough because it was owned by a relation.

The beautiful, picturesque Lake District, a national park and an area of sublime contrasts, where the majestic mountains and small crags have a seemingly timeless co-existence with lush greenery, calm lakes and gentle towns. Where, at ground level you are in natural amphitheatres, where you can watch the drama of the sky, as clouds move in ominously and cover the scene in rain, making the days of sunshine heavenly and blissful. And at the peaks, after hours of walking and climbing, you stand amongst those clouds and command views of sun dappled mountains and valleys. Until the clouds begin to shroud you in their cold mystery and you are forced to retreat to safety down below.

So I decided to move there to paint, to write, to just be creative. I believed that it was my last chance to nurture my talent, in a place where some of the greats of English Literature; Wordsworth, Coleridge and Ruskin, had found their inspiration. I wanted to commune with the Gods of Nature, with Pan and the elementals, though I found their nature in a different form.

I turned off the road from the lakeside town of Bowness-on-Windermere and drove between imposing, stone gateposts and up a gravel driveway. A beautiful meadow was to the left and tall rhododendron bushes to the right. A grand, neoclassical, Georgian mansion came into view at the end of the drive, whose access was closed off by a large iron gate. Unusual double CCTV cameras stared at me as I drove up to them, then I took a sharp right, onto a large gravel car park.

From here I carried my bags into a wooded area, up concrete stairs, stepping unevenly, to the top which opened into a courtyard of eight wooden lodges.

They looked solid, if somewhat basic, and were brightened by hanging baskets. I found mine by means of a slate plaque. It read "Swan Isle." My en-suite accommodation was surprisingly modern, with new but thin carpet and simple furniture.

The lodge smelt musty, masked by a cheap air-freshener which I promptly dropped in the bin. I also took from the walls the prints of brightly expressive paintings of flowers and cathedrals. My aim was to eventually replace them with some of my own daubs.

The lodge was cool in the shade of the trees so I was glad to be wearing a tweed jacket and jeans. I opened the French window doors onto the view, down through the trees to the jetty and the side of Lake Windermere. It wasn't ideal for painting, but the lodge was secluded, private. The picnic bench outside, on an uneven patio, was sodden so, in the lodge, I pulled a wide, green, leather couch around so that it faced out to the view.

I made a coffee and set up my laptop, to test the Wifi connection, and found I had an e-mail from my cousin, Rose. I was invited to tea, that afternoon, lucky I'd checked.

Then there I sat, starting to relax. The whirr of a motor boat passed. The birds chirped and the wind rustled in the trees.

That early-summer afternoon I headed to visit my cousin, by what she had told me was the quickest way, by taking the car on the Hawkshead ferry. I arrived at the side of the water, where the road just disappeared into the lake. The ferry was on the other bank, the flat water between us. Moored yachts and white houses peppered the hillside. Five minutes later the ferry returned to my side of the lake, navigated by an operator within a tower above the passenger cabin. Cars and walkers pulled out hastily and I was waved onto "Miss Westmorland" by an attendant in orange safety clothes. "And you'll be the first to make the mad dash when the barrier comes up," he said as he directed me to park at the front of the ferry. About ten cars had boarded behind me along with a motorbike and a group of walkers. The attendant came back to take my money in his bag.

The ferry shuddered as the cogs and cables moaned and the engine started to wind us across to the other side of the lake. Looking through the yellow barriers it was like surfing over the water. As we crossed the drivers got out and wandered around. I could see the great length of Windermere with the mountains at

Ambleside to the North. Then, after just five minutes, our cars spilled out of the ferry.

I drove warily on winding single track roads, bordered with hills, woods and dry stone walls. I half expected to meet drivers or walkers on the bends. The narrow roads were bursting with life from ground that was dry on the surface and damp underneath. The grass, bracken and ferns bustled onto the road. And occasionally there was a smell of wild garlic. The lakeside kept peeping through the trees and I was delighted to happen on the occasional idyllic cottage of slate and whitewashed lime.

I reached Xing and Rose's where a high slate wall ran the length of the estate. Huge trees and garbled mock Tudor gable ends were visible over the imposing wall. A hill sloped up behind me with a rocky outcrop. And a sign on the wall in front said 'CCTV monitored'. I announced my presence on an intercom and the metal gates opened.

I drove over the gravel driveway between two large concrete Chinese Dragon dogs, each seated with one foreleg raised, their mouths open, revealing menacing teeth. I passed a Chinese style low tiled roof garage, on which hung a stag's horns above the door, and parked next to a huge black Audi 4x4 and a red Ferrari. The house had steep-pitched, gabled roofs with a façade of white stucco and black timber. And I could see, through the hedges to the side of the house, that there was a swimming pool in the back garden.

On entering the house I expected to see suits of armour either side of a dark wooden hallway. Instead, it was a clinical white space with bright lights set into the ceiling. A complete transformation, and in the lounge a huge plasma screen tried to dominate the wall, beaten only by the view of the lake. It was a view created by knocking out the narrow Tudor windows to produce enough space for a giant window.

My cousin and her friend reclined on a white and chrome couch in the middle of the room. I recognised Rose from family functions years ago, though now she had blonde hair, coloured and cut in the latest style. She was matched by her friend, in black. Both wore slacks and t-shirts, though they had pristine make up and jewellery. The sun raked in through the window and allowed their gems to compliment, or compete, with the natural beauty of the sparkling lake outside. Her friend stopped looking at the view and Rose put down her I-pad. An over-fed black poodle with a gold tag in the shape of a bone wandered over to greet me.

Rose smiled. She gave a look that said she was happy, that I made her happy and that she wanted to share that happiness with me.

"So glad you could make it Dan. I didn't want you to feel all on your own over there. It must be years since we met, and look at you all dressed up, in tweed. We're just relaxing here. Qing zuo." She patted the space between them on the couch, the space that the dog had just vacated. "Come and join us." Despite the warm welcome she seemed curiously defensive. As though at once intoxicated by her own beauty, yet also unsure of it. Nevertheless she wielded power from the beauty she was confident in.

I felt awkward, so she got up, we hugged and then we sat. She put a hand on he side of my thigh. "My father says that he's sorry they had to lose you from the bank, but he was making cuts left right and centre and there would have been a big protest if none of the 'family' had taken any of the damage."

"That's fine, it gives me time to concentrate on what I really want to do." I fidgeted, taking off my jacket. I was fascinated by the fact that the only concessions to antiquity in the room was now a black screen hand painted and lacquered with Chinese birds and bamboo trees. That and two glazed porcelain Chinese Dragon dogs, smaller versions of the fierce looking ones outside. They guarded either side of the smooth black marble fireplace lit around with harsh blue L.E.D. lights. A broad stone chimney rose above the fireplace. Once the primary heating source for the home it was now merely ornamental.

"This is Becca Berezovsky," said Rose. "She's a good friend of mine. I met her in Shanghai, we were Postgraduates at University there."

I shook hands. "Oh really, what were you both studying?"

"I took a Masters in Chinese," said Rose.

"And did you learn Chinese as well?" I asked Becca.

Becca laughed. "I know enough Mandarin to get into trouble but not enough to get out of it," she spoke in a light Russian accent. "No, I did my Doctorate in Statistics and game theory in London. I was researching in China, and teaching."

"Are you Russian?" I asked.

"Her father is in Oil, dearest," said Rose. "He's what they like to call an oligarch. Which potentially makes her a future oligarchess. Dan here is a painter."

"Oh you must paint me," instructed Becca.

"Huh, excuse me. He's painting me first. And I insist I pay for it. And I've a friend in London, who owns a gallery, I'm sure he will add you to his stable of artists. Fancy, my portrait on exhibition in London. Before returning here, of course, to Zhang House."

"I couldn't, I'd feel a cheat. What about all the other artists?"

"Oh Dan, don't be silly. It's all about connections. You know that."

I couldn't accept it. All those talented artists who struggle for years, surviving on next to nothing and then can't find a gallery because it was full of work by those who were well connected. It seemed like my art would already be compromised if it wasn't tempered in the forge of critical review. "No, I'll paint you Rose, of course, but I'm not worried about a gallery at the moment, thank you." As I rejected the offer I wondered if other galleries existed where it wasn't all about who you knew.

"Do you make a living from painting?" asked Becca.

"I used to work in banking 'till the crisis," I replied.

"What in one of the cages, or something more managerial."

"No, in bonds," there was a pause, then I asked Becca, "What do you do?"

"I play Mah Jong, professionally."

"Oh, she's such a wiz," said Rose. "She plays Poker and Mah Jong Tournaments at Xing's Casino. The Chinese men can't believe how good she is and she beats them hands down."

"It's all statistics and psychology," said Becca.

"How do you play it anyway?"

"Oh how delightful," said Rose to Becca, "Dan doesn't know how to play Mah Jong. Let's play!" She turned to me, "It's like poker."

"I'll play. Only to show you how it's done," said Becca.

"Good, then I might have a chance of winning," said Rose. "It's easy Dan. You get thirteen tiles and from these you have to make sets of threes (pungs) fours (kongs) or sequences in the same suit (chows). If you get all your pieces you Mah Jong, go out."

"Will Xing be playing?" asked Becca.

"No, he's just in the gym," Rose explained. "You'll meet him later Dan. Oh, and I'll show you the gym at the side of the house and the pool at the back."

So a box of tiles was tipped onto the table and I spent the next hour learning the meaning of Chinese characters on small blocks of bamboo and bone. We "washed" the tiles face down on the table and then arranged them into four walls, each stacked two tiles high. We rolled dice and took our thirteen tiles. Selecting and discarding tiles I began to build my hand. I looked at the 'suits' of numbers, of circles, of bamboo, of winds and of dragons, admiring the beautiful simplicity of the designs. Our concentration led to a kind of peace in the room.

"You know, there's actually something very civilized and relaxing about playing games, like Mah Jong and cards," I suggested.

"It's the passing of the tiles between you. It's so seldom you get to share things these days. It's the exchange and barter," added Rose.

"Yes, and the better quality or more antique the set the better, all those years of play," added Becca.

Behind it, of course, was a desire to win. And just as I thought that I was getting somewhere I discarded a red dragon and Rose called "Mah Jong!" She lay her tiles, "I was waiting for that red dragon. There I've got three now, and 5,6,7 in bamboos, yi, er, san in numbers, three 5 circles and two North winds."

"Tai hao le. An auspicious pung to go out on, this being the year of the dragon, and red being the colour of good fortune." We all turned around, Xing had been watching us from the door. He stood in a sweat darkened grey vest. His hair was short and his face had an almost artificial symmetry. His cheekbones were very round and his eyes piercing. He was not tall, but his muscles were large and defined. It gave him presence.

"This is Xing, isn't he lovely. His father is an official in the Chinese Communist Party and runs a mobile phone company. His phone networks have helped transform commerce in Africa. And Xing's been helping him to make investments in the Lake District and Manchester." They speak to each other in Mandarin, Xing was clearly annoyed that he was described as secondary to his father.

He turned to me. "How are you finding the lodge, comfortable enough?"

I nodded.

"Good, how did you get here?"

"By car."

"I could've come across in the boat and collected you from the jetty. Oh well, maybe next time."

"Oh Dan, can you see your house from here?" asked Rose.

"No, it's in the trees," Xing replied.

"Maybe we can see the mansion next door," I suggested.

"No, all you can see is the jetty," said Xing. "Which reminds me, I must pay your," Xing gestured to me, "neighbour a visit sometime."

Rose tutted. "Silly me. Dan, you must be dying for a drink. Would you like some tea?"

I nodded and as she left I stood and looked out onto the garden and lawn, down to the lake. I could see three pointed, overly manicured, trees near the shore.

"Enjoying the view," says Xing, "I think I need to do something with those old trees. Spoils the view of my yacht, don't you think." He smiled like a small boy who wanted to get his own way.

"Not really," I replied, hiding disdain, "I rather like them."

"Ha. 'Plum Blossom' is a great boat, a really cosy cabin, isn't that right Rose, and a motor when you don't want to sail."

"That's a strange name for a boat," I suggested.

"Not really," he replied. "The plum blossom is the sweetness of winter, it flowers in the snow. It symbolises how beauty can come from hard times. That's why we Chinese like it. It reflects our character. And I call my boat 'Plum Blossom' because I'm going to sail her all year round."

Rose returned with a tray on which is a squat teapot and a number of small rounded cups and placed them on a low white table.

"I tried to organise the house along principles of Feng Shui," she said.

Xing laughed.

"The entrance energy needs channelling so that it doesn't just flow straight out of the house."

"Let's just pour and drink," joked Xing.

We all stood and she poured the tea. Bits of leaves floated in the cups. There was no milk or sugar. "Qing zuo," Rose said and we sat.

I admired the Chinese calligraphy on the sides of the cup and as soon as I finish my 'cha' it was filled again.

"Sorry it's a bit bare in here," said Xing. "We wanted to get back to basics, to a minimalism and start afresh. I collect modern art but I also fancy collecting original Chinese antiques. You are a painter, what do you think of that piece by Yue Minjun?" Xing pointed behind me and I turned to see the large, modern canvas of broadly smiling Chinese men with short hair. They were semi clad and on a bright background.

I cocked my head and raised an eyebrow and nodded. "Yeh, good." I didn't want to say what I really thought of the gaudy work.

"I've got a whole collection in the basement, just waiting to hang them. Fang Lijun, Zhang Xiaogang, Gu Wenda. The whole lot of them. Do you know Chinese artists?"

I shook my head as he rocked as if in pleasure that knowledge is power. "Not really my style," I added.

"So what is your style?"

At that point there was a buzz in the pocket of his sweatpants.

"Romantic through to Modernist. And Art Deco design of the 20s and 30s."

"Oh, I love that period," said Rose leaning forward.

"Ah, we'll have to talk later, I've got a business call I need to make," he replied as he rose from the table.

Outside we could hear "Wei" as he walks down the hall and the conversation got fainter.

"You know he never stops, he's so busy," says Rose. "And when he's not working he's working out in the gym or on his boat. I wish I was as fit as he is. I need to build a bit more muscle. Get rid of some of this flab," she grabbed her arm. "I need to do something with my hair as well. It's such a mess."

I had no idea why she was so critical of herself. She had everything and yet, at that moment, she really believed that she had nothing.

Xing returned, oblivious of the changed emotional landscape. "Dan, we should go to Manchester. I want to show you around a few places, and you never know, I may have a job for you. It can't be easy not having a salary any more. And I like to keep interesting opportunities open to members of my family."

"I'm fine, honestly."

"You say that, but in six months or a year's time you might change your mind and by then it could be too late. So let's spend a bit of time together, build our Guanxi, develop our relationship. Here, take my business card." Xing opened an elegant silver holder and offered me a card.

"Thank you. Sorry I can't return the card. I don't have any for my new line of work, at the moment."

"But you'll come with me won't you?"

My heart sank as I nodded. I had only just moved to get away from the quagmire of one City. And there I was, reluctantly agreeing to sink myself into another.

Chapter 2

ON THE WHOLE I'd brought clothes for the rugged Lake District, anticipating the occasional sunny spell, but mainly expecting it to be cold and wet. And whilst I had some more formal wear, suitable for a light business meeting, I thought that my jeans and a tweed jacket would keep me comfortably distant from the prospect of re-employment in a city. So this is what I wore when Xing picked me up in his 4X4. As we came into Bowness there were swans, pigeons and waddling ducks straying into the shore road. Xing drove through a group of swans, pushing them out of the way. This marked the beginning of his reckless behaviour. On the way to the motorway he took the corners recklessly and overtook on blind bends on uphill winding roads. He only faintly hid his enjoyment of my discomfort, acting as if his driving was normal, testing my reaction.

"You like football?" he asked, nonchalantly.

"I'm more a croquet player."

"I have season tickets for Manchester United. We can go sometime. I hardly use them." This marked the beginning of our failure to connect.

On the motorway we sped at 120 miles an hour, slowing down when his Sat-Nav warned of cameras and his electronic sensors picked up the police.

"I'm not sure you really like me," said Xing. "You seem to think you are in some way better than me. Well, don't blow your chances with me. If you want, you can have a place in my world. And I will pay you well. Rose has asked me to help you out, so I will. You have trading skills and I could use them."

"Yes, but I've left that behind, I'm trying to become a painter and writer now."

"Yes, yes, and when you change your mind this is how I can help you."

It felt like I was in a tiresome interview for a job that I didn't want from an employer who didn't particularly want me.

Nonetheless, I went through my employment history as we made our way to the M61 and finally drew nearer to Manchester. We passed through areas of decayed factories and the desolation of an unemployed industrial town. Drab, dirty, dusty streets underlay a landscape of motorways, tower blocks, broken factories and empty warehouses

"We're going to my Casino, another venture that I'm developing and refurbishing."

On the road coming into the city centre trees, visible beyond the advertising hoardings, grew from abandoned brick bridges. Row upon row of empty brick factories, converted into offices, were now empty again, dominated by the glass and steel which rose above this hard red landscape. Xing pointed out a high tower block. Its upper half, wider than the lower half, looked perilously overhanging.

"See that, it's Beetham Tower. The bottom half is the Hilton, the upper half is apartments. I own some of them."

Closer still and beige Georgian fronts mixed with cream art deco buildings, car parks, Victorian iron bridges, wasteland and modern structures in concrete cladding. We entered a warren of jostling monoliths and merged with the flow of taxis, buses, sports cars and delivery vans. Suited men and women walked briskly from lunch back to work, still pristinely made up for the days business but already looking forward to leaving. I was relieved not to be a part of it. And was determined not to get sucked back in.

I felt more relaxed when we turned into China Town where a giant three-tiered Dragon Gate spanned the road. We parked nearby. Its red columns on granite plinths supported ornate, golden roofs skirted with gilded filigrees. Red, turquoise and golden dragons, sat, perched on gable ends, watching. Double CCTV cameras overshadowed the Gate. They were unusual, like the cameras outside Gatsby's mansion.

Xing pointed to the cameras and laughed, "CCTV, closed circuit television, in China CCTV stands for China Central Television. The state watches everything."

A big sign nearby read 'These Premises and many others are protected by BTV Security, for a free, no obligation quote call...' "One of my friends runs that firm. Give him a wave," said Xing, his arm waving out of the window.

The sun shone on the cameras, bringing the eyes to life. They moved, following and tracking the cars and people on the streets.

We got out of the car. "Here's the Casino." 'Forbidden City' was on the sign across the front and etched onto the frosted windows. We went up steps, through a red gated door and into an entrance where there were two tall wooden seats carved with dragons. Across from these the receptionists bowed to Xing. "Nimen hao."

We entered into a plush carpeted area with people at the gaming tables and a bar in the corner.

"We have roulette tables, blackjack tables and gaming machines. We also run Poker and Mah Jong Tournaments." Old men and ladies sat around tables making loud clickety clacks.

"What's that noise?" I asked.

"Mah Jong tiles. They're all playing it over there. It's one of our innovations, Mah Jong Tournaments, but we have to get rid of its image as on old person's game. I'm making it a bit sexier, so that people will play for higher stakes." He pointed to an area behind frosted glass windows. "We have a restaurant as well. Though it has seen better days."

I looked through the glass doors. Red lanterns and Chinese style paintings of rural scenes lifted the attention from the chrome chairs and used table cloths. Xing seemed a bit embarrassed

"The casino is my main business here, and I'm renovating it. I want it to be my first of many." Then he saw a sultry blackjack dealer leave her table and wander over. She had a bright red mouth and porcelain white skin. She was very slim, with large cheekbones and eyes made bigger through strong makeup.

"Dan, this is Meihua, it means beautiful flower."

I remember realising that she must have been the person who Xing had been on the phone to. Meihua leaned over the table and smiled, offering her hand, which I reluctantly shook. Xing said "I'll see you at the Tower in an hour."

"I can't get away from the table."

"Close it and tell them you are on an errand for me."

"Okay tiger," she smiled and went to tidy up.

It felt like I was just Xing's excuse to be in Manchester. He was deceiving me as well as Rose. I shook my head in disdain.

"No need for superciliousness, Dan," he said, with superciliousness. "I'm done here, let's go."

So we left for the Hilton Tower, a short walk from the bustle of China Town. We entered the spacious and light entrance lobby and headed along a red carpet, past the reception, to an elevator with the logo of Cloud 23 above the door. A doorman called the lift. There were just 3 buttons in the lift. Xing pressed '23' and we quickly passed the first 22 floors of the tower.

The scene was commanding. "There are views across to the GMEX conference centre," said Xing. "The other side of the building looks over to green parks." A tall floor manager in a suit acknowledged Xing and looked stonily at me.

I couldn't understand why Xing had brought me here but it was surprisingly quiet. He ordered Daiquiri cocktails at the bar and then we crossed the room, escorted to our table by the haughty floor manager over a window in the floor. Xing stopped.

"Look, such a long way down," said Xing. I felt disorientated to look, yet the lines of the windows down to the courtyard and street below seemed to be so beautifully straight and simple. We then sat on curved red seats at a low table and looked across the cityscape.

"Gan Bei," said Xing, raising his glass.

"Gan Bei," I responded.

We drank and placed the glasses on a black marble table that contained fossils of ancient sea creatures. Xing opened his briefcase and got out a contract.

"Dan, this is strictly confidential. I want to start selling Chinese bonds, here in Manchester, and need someone with your experience to work for me. There's a good starting salary and you will be on performance related bonuses of course. The basic details and the fiscals are in here. But you will be creating your own position as well. So you'd pretty much have free reign to build the job as you see best. With my supervision of course."

"Sorry, I appreciate the offer," I was determined not to get sucked in, "but I'm just not interested at the moment. I want to be creative, painting and writing."

"Okay, but here are the details. And you'd be crazy to risk missing out on this opportunity."

"I'll see how I get along."

"Well, it won't wait forever."

"Nothing lasts forever," I remarked.

Xing finished his drink and banged the glass onto the table. "Okay, let's go to the apartment." Xing just upped and left and I found myself following, obediently.

We descended the tower and as the elevator doors opened a young business man stood in our way, expecting us to let him in. Xing marched out, brushing the man's shoulder and crashing his briefcase into the man's knee. Xing shook his head and said "Manners cost nothing."

Outside we turned the corner and entered to the Beetham Tower apartments, ascending until we got to Xing's floor.

Inside the apartment Meihua was there in a pink cocktail dress and large sunglasses. A young girl next to her looked uncomfortable in her dress. Chinese ornaments mixed in with luxuriant cushions and fur rugs. And a large golden Buddha and a large red dragon were positioned precariously on the mantelpiece.

"Ni hao Dan," said Meihua.

"I'd like you to meet Meihua's sister, Yingli," said Xing. "She's a nice girl for you." She looked softer and more vulnerable than Meihua. This was clearly her nature and lack of character deforming experiences. "Ni hao," she said. "Wo jiao Yingli."

"Ni hao," I replied. "Wo jiao Dan."

"Okay, let's party. Dan open the Champagne!"

I obliged, although I wasn't happy with the unorthodox situation.

I opened the Champagne and poured it.

"Gan Bei!" said everyone as we drank from the tall glasses. Next to the bottle, on a small table, by a vase of lilies was a statue of an old man with a staff. "Who's that?" I asked Meihua.

"That's Shou Lao with his peach, he gives me health and will help me to live to an old age." Meihua went over to her computer in the corner of the room.

"Look Dan," she said, "Wo ai wang gou. I love to buy off the internet." She showed me a a trinket box online. Then she went onto Facebook. "Wo jia ni wei haoyou. I add you as a friend." I realised that the Mandarin was for the benefit of her sister.

"Wode aihao shi Shangwang," said Yingli.

"Ha, she says she loves to surf the internet," said Xing. "You can give her something else to do Dan." He playfully punched my arm. Then we drank some more and looked at the items Meihua was planning on buying.

"You know, me and Meihua have lots in common. We both made mistakes."

I turned quizzically.

"Yes, though you said that you'd leave Rose for me." Her arms went around his shoulder. "So then we can be together and happy."

"We met at my Casino, Dan. As soon as I saw her I knew I had to have her. And of course, as soon as she saw me she couldn't keep her hands off me. Her husband is the chef there."

"Yes, he's no bother. And too dumb to know anything."

Her arms tightened and they kissed. Then Meihua took out a small gold box and emptied some white powder onto the table. Xing took a line, then Meihua. "Would you like some?" she enquired.

"No thanks," I replied. Then, when Yingli shook her head, Meihua spat words at her in Mandarin and the girl turned away.

"Where do you live Dan?" asked Meihua, weighing up the options for her sister.

"I'm from London, but I just moved to the Lake District."

"Yes, in one of my lodges."

"Oh, the lodges next to Gatsby's place?" asked Meihua. Xing turned his head sharply to her.

"I've no idea," I replied.

Xing laughed, "In my opinion that man is weak and decadent. He belongs to the past."

"Yes, but I want to go to one of the parties. They are becoming famous. But Xing won't let me," said Meihua as Yingli nodded in agreement, unsure what she was nodding to. "All the Manchester 'in' crowd go up to them. They are like old fashioned but smarter than anything new. We should all go and stay in one of your lodges."

"Well, what's wrong with our party here?" Xing asked. "Aren't they enough. I mean, I give you everything you want. And you fill the apartment with kitsch. This is more like what I want to collect" said Xing, going to the sideboard. "Proper Chinese culture, a blue and white Lotus Temple Vase, Ming Dynasty, Chenghua Period. Worth a fortune, I don't know why I keep it here. You just surround it with all this. And where do you get all this stuff anyway? Ebay, and Taobao. It's all worthless reproductions, you can't resell any of this stuff. It's junk."

"It reminds me of home."

"This is your home, and its also my home, and I don't want it filling with junk."

"Well it's not junk. And to be honest, it doesn't feel like home. You're never here. I want to be with you Xing. And there are lots of Chinese restaurants in the Lake District. You could get me a job in one of those, or start a casino or something."

"I give you all the money you need, what are you complaining about?"

"I'm no prostitute."

"No? Well your family seems pretty good at it. With you asking me if I can introduce your sister to someone."

Her eyes flashed hatred as she tried to scratch his face. So he carried her by the wrists, kicking, into the other room. From there she started to scream and cry out "No!! Bu Shi!!"

By the time the sobbing turned into laughing I had already resolved to leave. Yingli looked disturbed but didn't want to go. Waiting obediently for her sister.

"How old are you?" I asked. She didn't understand, so I had to sign and count my own age on my fingers for her.

She replied with her fingers and I counted. "Fifteen."

I didn't want to leaver her alone, but it was late, I was drunk and I couldn't stand being there a minute longer.

So I wandered off into the streets of Manchester, avoiding the drunken gangs and the screaming girls until I found a quiet bar by the canal. There I just sat, drinking, staying warm and dwelling on how I could have lived in a city for so long. How grateful I was to have managed to escape.

I was wakened by the barman at closing time, in the early hours. He pointed me to an all night café, by Piccadilly station, which I staggered to and remained, inconspicuously in the corner, nursing a cup of coffee, until I knew the train station would open. There I waited until I could catch the early train to Oxenholme. Then I got the connection to Windermere and from there a Taxi home, at last, to "Swan Lake".

Chapter 3

I FORGOT ABOUT my meeting with Xing, though his shadow never fully passed from my time in 'Swan Isle.' I soon settled into a routine. The lodge was bright and my mornings began early, with my taking cup of tea out to the bench when the weather was fine. I enjoyed it, in peace and quiet, looking down through the woods to the lake. It was completely idyllic. One morning, when I was up earlier than usual, I heard a swimmer before I saw him near the jetty on the lakeside. He emerged from the lake, tanned and muscled, in a full length black swimming costume, like the woollen ones that they wore in the 1920s. I guessed that it was Gatsby, the owner of the mansion, and that he must have swum from this side to the other, and back. His swim was a punctual event. I could almost time his appearance every other morning.

That was all I ever saw of him in the early days. Days occupied with reading and walking, sketching the Lakeland scenes I found or painting them, in-situ, with watercolours. I had been busy settling in to this new, creative existence and had not expected to find myself, one evening, exploring my 'neighbour's' mansion in the most interesting way.

Black 4x4s and roadster sports cars arrived, passing through the gates and then overspilling, to fill the car park near the lodges. I came out to look at some of the vehicles, Aston Martins, Morgans, Bentleys, Ferraris, Porsches, Land Rovers, BMWs...

The visitors got out of their vehicles. The men wore dinner suits and had slicked back hair. The ladies dressed as Flappers from the 1920's, wearing beaded or tasselled dresses and silk gowns. Some wore cloche hats and others had beaded, feathered headbands. They carried fur trims, wrapped over long gloved arms. And their necklaces and ear rings sparkled.

The group of guests gathered and just seemed to sweep me along. I wasn't at all dressed for the part but I joined the crowd and as we waited to get through the gate one of them remarked,

"I wish I was staying in the mansion," and another added, "And I wish Gatsby's butler could've ferried us from our hotel in that car." I hid my face from the twin CCTV cameras as I listened.

"Does he really think that he's the Great Gatsby?" asked one young girl.

"Who cares as long as he puts on these parties," replied her escort.

"How can he afford it all?"

"Don't ask where he gets all his money from. It can't just be antiques and property. But don't think about it, just enjoy the party."

"I heard that he really thinks he is the Great Gatsby character, from the novel by F. Scott Fitzgerald."

"The whole thing seems a bit sinister."

"I think it's rather romantic."

An old car drew up behind us. It looked like a Rolls Royce, but had a different mascot. Its low, wide body and large lamps spoke of an elegant age long gone. We moved out of its way and followed it up the drive as the gate opened. Its number plate read GAT 58Y. I was entering one of the famous 1920's themed parties of the so called Great Gatsby.

We followed it to the entrance porch, a colonnade of four Doric pillars, that supported a plain parapet of stone lotus buds. The house had beautifully large sash windows, either side of which were thick scrolled brackets that supported triangular pediments. The doors under the porch were guarded by a couple of sturdy looking fellows who waved on the crowd and then started talking to the chauffeur, in his jodhpurs and hat. We all headed towards a large marquee at the side of the house.

A boat was just arriving with an onboard jazz band playing, disturbing the lake. A mass of people called from the decks and waved hands out of the sides. "He chartered the boat for a jazz cruise," said one of the guests. The passengers alighted and it was as if our two groups approached the house from both flanks, like the barbarian hordes at the gates of Rome.

"Come on, we should be in time for the Burlesque acts."

"They won't start until the Jazz Band gets there."

A group of young musician alighted from the boat onto the jetty. Their thinness was chic and the leader wore perfectly round glasses.

Our merged mass headed around to the front of the house. Past the marquee tent, past the lush greenery, the Japanese red maple, the monkey puzzle trees, giant conifers and enormous rhododendron bushes. Onto the nicely mown lawns bordered by ferns topiaried into box bushes. There stood the mansion, in its elegant glory, looked like a simple classical villa, from the late 1700s but with a beautiful dome in its centre. The building also had a new looking extension to house extra guests. I say "new", but it was at least 150 years old.

On its terrace large urns with flowering plants were precisely placed, bordering the wooden tables and chairs. Guests scrambled to get the best views and sitting positions. Sitting like peacocks, preparing stories of their privileged vistas to brag about to friends on future 'occasions'. Two, giant, stone horses head chess pieces flanked the steps from the terrace to the rolling lawn that fell down to the lake's edge, bounded by trees on either side. Laughter and the clack of croquet balls came from the lawn. And a young man made much of the fact that he had stumbled over one of the hoops. But all this paled to insignificance as I found my spot.

The panoramic view from the lawn out to the lake was magnificent. The sun raked across the forests and hazy mountains that stood, in the distance, beyond the clear lake. Sparkling diamonds bobbed on the water. A reflection on the murky, unclean water below. But it was still the Diamond Lake.

On the terrace I discovered that the guests were from Manchester, London and even further abroad. There were Americans, Asians, Arabs, Africans, Latinos, Orientals and all were unified by Gatsby's strict dress code, vintage 1920's and 30's. And if it wasn't the doormen who maintained sartorial decorum then the guests themselves had been know to throw a man in the lake for wearing jeans. So I found a table at which to sit, inconspicuously, in order to hide my fashion faux pas.

The guests seemed to include High Society and also the stars of celebrity culture and reality TV. You could tell who the 'Stars' were, they were the ones less interested in seeing than in being seen. Ladies in bead and pearl necklaces, headbands, feathers and sequin patterned dresses mixed with men in dinner suits or dressed like Chicago gangsters in pin-stripe suits and fedora hats. There was even a couple of men with monocles, white bow ties, top hats and tails. Their names were Mr Pranab Rajaratnam and Mr Rajat Mukherjee, both investment consultants from Mumbai, a fact I discovered as they went around introducing themselves, handing their business cards around.

I noticed that some of the guests had real fur, the heads and tails of foxes and minks draped either side of their shoulders. It all seemed like a fine balancing act that had tipped dangerously far beyond taste. Some guests were dressed with turbans and saris like princes and princesses of the Raj. And fez's as if they were Egyptian visitors from the long gone days of the colonial British Empire. A handsome young black man came to ask what I would like to drink. He was dressed in a red dinner jacket and looked like a colonial servant. A gold badge on his lapel had the name 'Dwayne.' The party quietened and I asked for a glass of champagne. Dwayne needed my credit card. I gave it and turned to face the house.

The music of 'Swan Lake' began and a burlesque lady, with a white feather head-dress began to dance holding two huge fans, the size of her body. She made her way over the grass, down to the lakeside. Where she used the fans to emulate the appearance of a swan to the stunning backdrop of the lake. With great adeptness she slowly removed clothes until she was hidden completely naked behind the feathers. She made her way back to the house and then disappeared on finally, 'tantalisingly' revealing the jewelled cap coverings on her nipples and knickers.

The burlesque model then came back out and posed as cameramen and women took photographs. She had now covered her, clearly augmented, breasts and was seeming oblivious of the concept of a 1920's era of straight, boyish, body lines. I observed the scene as my drink arrived, served in wide and shallow champagne glasses. Beautifully etched.

The night went on and the terrace was then taken over by the Jazz band and its bespectacled leader. Apparently he was a famous trumpeter, though I had no idea who he was. The sounds were so mellifluous and graceful, then dived into raw energy and improvisation. People danced the Foxtrot, the Tango and the Waltz. But most of all they danced the Charleston. Big groups all doing the same moves, arms flailing, legs kicking and heads knocked back in laughter.

The moon was bright and the sky began to cloud over as the sun set. As soon as a chill set in the ladies rushed in to grab their fur coats to return displaying added glamour. A huge champagne glass was brought out and the burlesque dancer began to take off fur and chiffon layers. Glittering tassels remained and then she climbed into the glass, the water glistening on her legs as she stretched them into the air.

"She must be freezing," said the lady next to me. I turned and was surprised. It was Becca. She looked elegant in a drop waist beaded dress.

"Oh Dan, what are you doing here, who invited you? I guess it must've been Gatsby. I've just been chatting with him. He wants me to help him with his poker some time. Anyway, I still want you to paint me you know."

I nodded, changing the subject, "Who are all these people?"

"Hedge Fund Managers, accountants, fashion designers, artists, writers, television producers, footballers, media people from the BBC, writers, doctors, high paid council officers, civil servants, politicians, anyone with money really."

"Are they just here to party?" I asked.

"They come for sailing, riding, shooting, walking, climbing, cycling, whatever. He lets them stay, provided they pay a price and dress the part. You know, wearing tweeds, like country gents in the day and dressing glamorously in the evenings. And when they come he throws these huge parties. And people drink champagne and cocktails, and there are little areas where they take other things, or meet "friends". But he doesn't touch anything when he is running a party. And he isn't really present. People think he's being elusive and mysterious. But he's just too busy organising everything."

"They seem to come from all around the world."

"Sure do. Look, why don't I show you inside?" she suggested. As I stood up she quickly added, "Oh Dan, how could you. Jeans. I take it you haven't ended up in the lake yet. You're such a rebel," she laughed.

We sidled our way past the guests into the dining room where glistening crystal chandeliers competed for my attention with the gambling around a roulette wheel on the main table. Big mirrors reflected the antics of the guests, lit by the chandeliers and by lamps held aloft by classical bronzes of young boys. I looked around. The mansion was carpeted in red, the walls a strangely soothing mustard yellow. Paintings of Lakeland scenes and aristocratic ladies hung in heavy gilded frames. And big propeller fans spun upon the ceiling.

"Only invited guests have a room in the house, ones that he takes to look at properties in the Lakes. And all the antiques are for sale, though if you need to ask the price you wouldn't be able to afford them. He has cameras operating in the rooms," she pointed to a small round ball above the door, a CCTV camera, "to make sure any damages are paid for and nothing goes missing. The objects in the house are numbered, with tags and stickers. They are lots for auction and everything in the house can be viewed on-line. Every month he throws a big party. Items are then sold by auction and the house is then restocked with antiques by the Johnson-Smythes in Manchester."

I pushed my way through the crowds to Gatsby's tall bar, taken from some old music hall or other. Here they were selling Champagne and Long Island Iced Tea. The 'tea' was poured out of a teapot onto crushed ice in a tea cup. The barman told me "It's vodka, gin, white rum, lemon juice, sugar syrup and cola. They used to serve it in teacups to hide it from the Feds in the Prohibition era, when alcohol was illegal."

I bought Becca and myself a 'tea' and talked about games and social dynamics. It turned out that she didn't know how to play croquet. A game I grew up with and honed to a fine art at Oxford. We exchanged numbers and she insisted that she would arrange for us to play on Gatsby's lawn one afternoon.

Becca then excused herself, saying that she needed to chat with a few friends, so I took my cup and saucer and found a vacant high-backed chair. There were many, of various styles and upholsteries, mostly occupied. I found one and put my drink onto a beautifully carved and polished wooden table, protected by a glass top. Reclining on the couch, I looked at the ornate plasterwork around the high ceilings. Behind me the mechanics of a grandfather clock whirred into life and it chimed, surprising me.

A sign into an adjoining room, where an old silent movie was being projected, read 'Joan Crawford in 'Our Dancing Daughters' and Clara Bow in 'Plastic Age.'' A camp looking man came out of a room with white powder around his nose. An older man nearby looked shocked. "What's the big deal?" said the camp man to him. "Alcohol was illegal in 1920's Prohibition, you had to go to a Speakeasy to drink it. Well this is just the modern prohibition.!"

"Postmodern actually" I thought, but didn't see the point to mention it.

A boisterous group of young men and ladies came into the room. As they larked around one of them began eyeing my jeans so I rose and looked for a quiet place, to take a rest from the vacuous spectacle. I entered the library and started to peruse the books on poetry and art. I was startled at a rustle and almost dropped a first edition of Humbert Wolfe's 'The Uncelestial City.' A man was sitting, not three feet away from me, in a high backed leather chair. He was dressed in a black silk bow tie and button braces, and his hair was swept back, slicked down with pomade and parted at the side. Few men have ever made me swoon, but his demeanour was compelling.

"What's your name, old sport?" he asked. He looked at me with a quality of complete valuing.

"Dan, and you?" I replied.

"Just call me Gatsby. That's how I like to be known."

Gatsby crossed his legs, his white spats now on display. He seemed contradictory. A tough, hardened man, yet gentle, an aesthete. He nodded at the book I was holding. "Humbert Wolfe, let me read you my favourite of his." He rose and took a book from the shelf and began to read from "The Locri Faun":

'But even so the tune draws on!
when love is done, when love is done,
the tune is love, the tune the lover,
and the grass on the grave when love is over,
and, where this love is sacrificed,
the tune breaks round the feet of Christ.

The heart of man is the Creator
for ever than his own gods greater,
and even the truth that he has made
in his own image–Christ-will fade,
where gold, beyond the gold of dawn,
listen! The reed, and see! The Faun!

Let him stand in every cool
garden straight and beautiful,
secret in the heart of man,
the unassuageable shape of Pan,
who was all things, who is all things
and has no wings, and needs no wings.'

He closed the book and we were silent for a few moments.

"Yes, profound." I breathed deeply, changing my composure. "He was my great grand uncle."

"Really, I enjoy his work immensely. Do you know the work of the Lakeland poets?" he asked.

"'Fair seed-time had my soul, and I grew up Fostered alike by beauty and by fear,'" I recited.

"Wordsworth's The Prelude," he replied. Then retorted 'Bliss was it in that dawn to be alive, But to be young was very heaven!'"

"The same," I replied then retorted:

'In Xanadu did Kubla Khan
a stately pleasure-dome decree,
where Alph, the sacred river, ran
through caverns measureless to man
down to a sunless sea,'

but before Gatsby could say Coleridge's name I added, "I guess this is all your pleasure-dome."

"I try to create a little bit of utopia in an increasingly dystopic world," he replied.

I wandered over to the fiction and found a number of editions of 'The Great Gatsby'. "But this must be your favourite book," I suggested.

"It's certainly the most influential on me. But the difference between myself and the Gatsby character is that, at heart, he is a bit more of an ordered Apollo, whereas I'm a bit more of a wild Dionysus. He aimed for an intense experience of becoming, rather than a natural being. Whereas I believe that intense experiences of perfection can help us see the perfection behind everything in nature, even the dullest, most insignificant part. They help us accept that we are part of a natural being. And then we can realise that we are one with everything, eternally."

"So how's that fit with your partying?" I asked, unconvinced.

"I just do this because it's where I am, at this moment in time. But it has no more ultimate meaning for me than anything else. I just play out this as a role. I avoid getting trapped into believing any of the dreams we create for ourselves are ultimately real. And I like the aesthetics of people, like my books. I collect them, old sport, but I don't necessarily get involved with them all. Just like I don't read all these," he gestured to the books. "And some of my favourites aren't even in English. I have illuminated manuscripts, early Bibles, copies of the Koran and the Bhagavad Gita."

I laughed. "That reminds me of the Groucho Marx quote. 'From the moment I picked your book up until I put it down I was convulsed with laughter. Some day I intend reading it."
Gatsby laughed

"How are you enjoying the party?" he asked.

"I mean, your party and house and everything seems great, but something doesn't sit well with me. We left a lot of bad things behind in the past. What about the furs of your guests and your colonialist, psuedo racist attitudes to serving staff?"

"Attitudes were different in the 20s. And I can only choose what people wear to a certain extent," he smiled at my jeans. "And Dwayne, he's my personal assistant, and head waiter, he enjoys the work, and the dressing up. And I pay him well. And the guests know I won't tolerate any abuse. In fact, I can watch whatever goes on."

Gatsby showed me a room, next to the library, with a bank of television screens. Here he could watch over all his antiques and he showed me how, if any were moved, his sensors would notify him on his mobile phone.

I looked at the screens then blurted out, "Too many people, all fighting for attention. It's like big brother, celebrity culture gone mad."

"The problem isn't celebrity culture and everyone wanting to be a star. It's just that people want to be listened to and valued for who they are. But no one listens any more, so the only way to have a voice is to become famous, or know someone famous, even if just for a moment."

I shook my head, unsure what I thought about it all.

"Where are you staying?" asked Gatsby.

"In one of the lodges, by your car park," I replied.

"Ah, yes, I know the owner, Xing. And how did you come to stay there?"

"Oh, he's married to my cousin. They knew I needed somewhere to stay in the Lakes."

Gatsby looked very interested, but his mobile rang. "Sorry," he answers it. "Yes, New York? Alright, put it in an e-mail and I'll look at it tomorrow." He hung up.

"So, Mr Gatsby, what line of business are you are in?" I asked

"I'm in the nostalgia business."

"How can it be nostalgia if your guests never lived in that era in the first place."

"Let's say, nostalgia can be about being comfortable enough to forget what really is your past."

I decided I had had enough philosophy and too much to drink to continue the debate.

"I saw that you have a croquet lawn."

"Yes, do you play?" asked Gatsby.

"I used to be in the croquet club at Oxford."

"Splendid. Perhaps we can play sometime."

"Yes, Becca said she would try and arrange so I could teach her on your lawn."

"Oh, she did, good. Well feel free to use my set whilst you're staying in the lodges. Its nice to have someone here who knows how to play. I'm more a swimmer and a hiker at the moment but I'd like to learn myself someday."

"How far do you swim in the mornings," I asked.

"Oh, one side to the other and back, every other day."

"How long does it take?"

"Oh, not long. Anyway, I'd better make an appearance outside." Gatsby put on his double breasted jacket and his fedora hat. He went to the mirror, then adjusted the hat and the handkerchief in his breast pocket. "Enjoy your reading Dan. I'm sure we'll meet again. And next time, please feel invited to come to my party, in suitable attire."

Outside the party had reached the last stages of raging. The guests began to leave by chauffeur, taxi and some were even driving themselves. Surely they were over the drinking limit but seemed to assume the police wouldn't be bothered around here. And as the group thinned out various personalities took the opportunities to monopolise the conversations that arose. A middle aged man was babbling to a group of much younger ladies about how great he was, how much he had. Like so many of the guests he turned the conversation to salaries, bonuses, shares, who he'd slept with, TV appearances and who he knew.

I wasn't sure that I'd ever want to return to Gatsby's place. I felt like I was here for something more profound than partying. But over the next few days I tried but failed to write and paint. I walked in the mountains and beside the lakes but I received no inspiration. It was as if all that was original here had already been done and said. And it rained. It was then that the Lakeland Mountains surrounded me with their cold, grey presence. Their peaks now took on a different mood, reminding me that they were formed of brutal, volcanic rock. But all nature's majesty had been expressed and it was just more of the same. A change was needed, something that was outside of my control.

There was a curtain, a sheet of rain as I wandered around the town of Bowness. The sky was a uniform grey and the rain made a haze of the view. But the town was still busy, a sea of umbrellas. It was full of people who drove to the Lake District, then parked for a couple of hours, went to the shore, wandered around a few shops, had something to eat and drink, then drove back home. At the water's edge steamers and small boats took passengers as swans floated in from the lake, eyes hidden by dark markings. Their dignity seemed stripped as they waited to be fed by the teasing tourists.

I tried feeding ducks and visiting hotels, bars and coffee shops. It seemed like that was all there was to do in the rain. And in the evenings I would go where the hotel waiters, cooks, receptionists and bar staff would go out and get drunk. Then at the weekend they would mingle with the young visitors who would come to drink and meet people for casual sex.

That was how it seemed, and although there were plenty of Polish workers not many of them went out. They were more interested in sending their low wages home to their families in Poland. Supposedly working harder than the local people, many of whom had become unemployed, on benefits, or had moved to cities like Manchester. Moving to find somewhere cheap enough to live because the wealthy people from Manchester, London and further away, were buying up their family houses to turn them into casual holiday homes, empty most of the year.

So I found myself avoiding that world and drifted into a relationship with Becca. And that's what took me back to Gatsby's mansion, her wish to play croquet on his lawn when the weather was good. The house always remained closed to us in the day, all except the conservatory, so that we could retrieve the croquet set. And I never really saw Gatsby, but Becca assured me that he'd said it was alright.

We carried the stand out and set up the peg in the middle of the rectangular lawn, six hoops around it. Then we took the balls, I'd play blue and black, Becca played red and yellow. The lawn had a slant which made the game more sporting, easier to jump balls and send the opposition the other side of the pitch.

"I'll thrash you within an inch of your life," Becca kept insisting. She was ruthless at the game and turned it into some kind of business analysis, so I knew that I shouldn't get involved with her. I guess it was just physical attraction and loneliness. That and wanting to know more about her psychology.

"Your Doctorate in Game Theory, what is it actually?" I asked.

"Oh, just seeing when the rules that you have in games also apply in life and business situations, so that you can work out the best way to play."

"So what does it tell you about life then?"

"Well, there are rules for getting on together," she explained, "and they would work if it wasn't for the people who don't want to follow them. The psychopaths. They only make up a tiny minority of the population, but a huge number of business leaders have psychopathic traits."

"That doesn't surprise me."

"Yes, and they mess it up for everyone else."

"Sounds right," I added with a glint in my eye, as I croquet her ball off to the other side of the lawn.

"Take Xing, he wants to compromise you, so he can have you in his pocket. I don't know how he'll do it, but he will."

"He's already tried."

"What do you mean."

"Oh, something, in Manchester. But I wouldn't play ball."

"I'll bet he was angry," she said.

"I haven't spoken to him since."

The weeks went on and I painted Becca's portrait, as a commission. She had cajoled me into doing it, when I had wanted to paint the landscape. She said that she wanted to be famous and wanted before and after portraits.

"Famous for what?" I asked her.

"Oh, anything really." she replied.

I painted her against the plain wall of my lodge. And when I had finished I wasn't happy with the work.

"Sorry, its not very good."

"It's great, and besides, you had to rush it. It doesn't do justice to your talents."

"No, I'd like to be able to paint more effortlessly."

"Why don't you just take photographs and work from them. I know the old Masters didn't do it but artists like Salvador Dali used photos."

"It's easy to paint from a photograph," I said, "but when you paint from life you are more involved with the subject, you can develop an emotional connection and expression in the work."

And to be honest, this had been the problem, I had been happy with it a number of times but because I knew that Becca would have disapproved of the image, because I hadn't made her look beautiful enough, I changed what had worked. What had been a collection of simple brush strokes was turned into an overworked mess.

And in a way, I was glad it hadn't worked because she had expected it for free. Like it was payment to her for having a relationship with me, or she had wanted me to be so in love with her that I would offer it for free. If she'd told me she wouldn't pay I wouldn't have done it as I would have preferred to focus on the general landscape of beauty, rather than work, meticulously on one individual part within it. A part whose real beauty I was becoming increasingly unsure of.

Chapter 4

I GUESS, INADVERTANTLY, I could blame the croquet. An innocent game that led me back to the distasteful social games and exhibitionisms at Gatsby's place. But it was Becca who persuaded me to attend Gatsby's parties again, as her 'chaperone', not that she needed one.

I'd like to tell you about some of the regular guests and the antics they got up to, only I can't mention their names for fear of the tiresome, additional inconvenience of Lawsuits – although I'm sure they were Tweeted about and posted on Facebook at the time. They included lawyers, barristers, stockbrokers, antique collectors, business people, dancers, celebrities, aristocrats, civil servants. People connected with the movies and TV and social networking sites. And then there were the people that you will have heard of in the later press scandals. Edward Johnson who had multiple affairs and divorced later in the year. Paul Rothschild who lost his job for his 'activities.' The unfortunate Jane Hamlyn, who committed suicide, her double life exposed. Sir Richard Henson who killed his wife. Dr Mark Goldsmith who had a horrific car crash. George Morgan, a rogue trader with four billion in losses, now in prison. Mike Bergoine the footballer with a cocaine and spending habit. All this and yet everything seemed like a relatively innocent, if somewhat distasteful, game on our side of the lake.

Gatsby invited me to play croquet one morning, or rather teach him how to play. It was damp, but I still came to play. He had dropped off a striped boating blazer, a white shirt, white flannels and white shoes, all in my size. With them came instructions, on Gatsby headed invitation paper. 'Hi Dan, left these so that we can both be suitably attired for croquet in the morning and boating in the afternoon. Till then - Gatsby.'

I was early and the house was closed. So I wandered around the grounds, over the lawns and down to the lake. A flock of geese took to the air in startled unison as I approached.

The house was built on a corner of land that jutted out into Windermere and an area of woodland separated the south lawn from the jetty to the west of the house. I followed a path that led between the lawn and the jetty, through the woods. Halfway along this, at a lakeside clearing, was a walkway out into the water.

At the end of this walkway was an octagonal tower, with an arched entrance and three arched open windows. Gatsby stood in the tower. As I started up the walkway he turned, embarrassed, "Sorry old sport, is that the time?" He came out to lead me back down the walkway. As if to block me from seeing that he had been looking from its western window across the water, towards the three trees at Xing and Rose's. "Do you like the Temple, it was dedicated to four Admirals of the navy." I nodded as we headed back to the house.

As we came out of the woods there were rabbits on the lawn. "If you're extra quiet," he said, "you can see deer. They just wander up."

It was now drizzling on the lake and was heading our way. "Not much croquet happening today, what with the weather," I said.

"It'll be fine, we can get a few hoops in before lunch," he insisted.

We headed up to the house and entered the narrow orange and white conservatory. Its walls ran parallel to the outside of the dining room walls and its windows were bounded at the sides with trestles. In this terracotta floor tiled space was a life-size terracotta statue of Pan. I could see his goat waist and legs. His flute was missing from his hands, presumably a gilded flute, perhaps stolen as a memento by an opportune guest. We sat on wicker chairs and Gatsby opened the tall French windows to view down the gravel terrace to the lake. Next to us were white plinths with Corinthian capitals, contrasting delightfully with the terracotta urns and floor tiles. Small orange trees stood next to two small white sphinxes and two large Chinese urns.

Dwayne appeared, with a tray of Tea in a silver pot, biscuits and fine china ware. Next to Gatsby, on a table, sat a beautiful gold phone, with green marble handle, on a gold stand and green marble base. Over the course of tea it would ring and Gatsby would take business calls from New York, Moscow, Mumbai London and Rio de Janeiro.

The light rain passed and the sun came out, so we were ready to play. Gatsby opened a black box. "HMV 101," he remarked, "early 1930's, you just don't get the same sound with digital." He set up the wind up gramophone in the conservatory so that we could hear it as we played. Though he would later keep going back to wind it up, playing the same shellac 78 record.

"This is my favourite tune at the moment. The Sheikh of Araby, inspired by the Rudolph Valentino silent movie where Valentino steals a woman away from her room and to his tent in the desert, where she becomes his lover. In the 1920s the ladies were called Flappers and the men were called Sheikh's."

'Well I'm the Sheikh of Araby,
your love belongs to me.
Well at night where you're asleep,
into your tent I'll creep.
The stars that shine above
will light our way to love.
You rule this world with me,
I'm the Sheikh of Araby.'

Gatsby put on a Panama hat with a black band and ridge over the top and we commenced play. The balls picked up grass as they rolled on the fresh cut lawn. Although he clearly knew the game already he wasn't at all a ruthless player, and I got the feeling that he didn't play to his full ability. However, I showed him a few tricks, like how to jump the balls over each other.

Gatsby folded his Panama and put it in his pocket as he went to enter the house. "Thank you Dan. That was most useful. I don't know about you, but I'm a bit peckish. I think we should have a spot of lunch, on the lake."

Dwayne brought us a picnic hamper and we headed to the jetty, where an old wooden motor boat was moored. On the side of the boat was painted 'Vivian.' We climbed in and the boat rocked.

"Vivian is 80 years old," he said as he put her in reverse and turned the steering wheel. He pushed back the roof and I lounged in the back as we cut through the water at a leisurely pace. Occasionally we would be rocked by the waves from a passing yacht. The clouds were very low, or was it that the mountains were high.

Gatsby cut the engine in the middle of the lake. Whilst we drifted the sun found an extended break in the clouds and began to bathe us in its glory.

"Alright, picnic time," said Gatsby opening the hamper. "okay, Champagne, glasses, sandwiches, scones. I know what I'd like first. I don't often get chance to have a drink, always have to stay aware and watch everyone else. But would you join me?"

I nodded, it seemed a bit of a rare privilege. He fired the cork into the sky then poured into the delicate glasses and we savoured the delicate flavours. "Here's to you Dan," he said. "To your new beginning."

"And to you, who ever you are," I laughed.

A breeze picked up. The sweat cooled upon my back and cloud began to obscure the sun again. The sun struggled to break back through and suddenly it began to rain. Then we were riding in the rain. Soaking wet, the boat slowly filling with rain water. We were laughing as we headed over to the three pointed trees outside Xing and Rose's mansion. I'd never seen the boat house next to them but their whole estate was easily visible from the lake. I felt voyeuristic as we gazed. "Someone's coming out," I said, and so we span round on the water and headed back into the lake.

Myself and Gatsby were jubilant. Life doesn't get any better than this. It seemed like maybe there should have been something more, but if that was all there was then that was fine. It was as much as I needed.

Gatsby was never out of control and in measured time we headed back to the jetty.

"I'd like to invite you to come to Manchester with me tomorrow To have a look at some of the things I do. I think you'd find them really interesting. I'm having the auction of the items from the house. And I have to select some more stock. And the forecast is good, so we can go in the Beauford."

"Spiffing," I said, as I raised my glass.

The next day the sky was clear and it was beautifully sunny. I headed over to Gatsby's in Chinos and a blue blazer. He stood outside the house, in front of his Beauford, in a beige suit, brown brogues, a pale fern shirt and sky blue tie. The car was pure 'Art Deco,' with arches that swept down into running boards. I walked around the car. It had whitewall tyres and a spare whitewall wheel on the side. Chrome headlights stared out from below the winged mascot. An old Automobile Association badge at the front completed the look.

"What kind of car is it?"

"It's a Beauford. A modern version of a 1920's Rolls Royce and a 1929 Dusenberg. Difference is I can use it all the time, without ruining its value. It's got a fibre glass and alloy body, built onto a Ford Sierra running gear and with a Rover V8, 3.5 litre engine."

"It's fantastic, takes you to a bygone era."

"This is the car I taxi guests in, and sometimes do weddings with."

"Do you do many?"

"Enough for the taxman," he said as he put on a light baker boy driving cap, to protect his slicked back hair. And round sunglasses, with leather protectors at the sides.

The car had four doors. I stepped on the running board as I got into the car and the plush black leather seat creaked as it yielded to my weight. It wasn't long, in the wind protection of the car, before sweat wet my trousers, shirt and jacket. I took off my jacket and my arms stuck to the leather of the car. And then we headed down the drive.

We drove the same route that Xing had taken, only slower, more enjoyable. It was like being in some old film, the winged mascot at the front of the car cutting the air before us. Being driven in the Beauford was so blissfully cooling. "When it is sunny in the Lakes it's like Eden. I can't imagine anywhere that I'd rather be," called Gatsby.

We drove between the cool and the heat on shade dappled roads. Down smooth, winding roads, inside tunnels of green life, with sun drenched expanses of green lushness. Then emerged onto a vista of a vast expanse of water, bordered by mountains, backed with clear blue skies. And on this expanse brilliant white masts of bobbing boats jostled for attention.

I sweated in the sun but the fresh wind blew my body. It was a pleasurable balm. We overtook the shadows of clouds that passed over sun bathed hills. And I watched as the wind stroked the grass, creating rippling waves.

Just before the M6 junction Gatsby stopped the car and got out to put the leather hood up, fastening it at the sides. Then we headed onto the M6 and down to Manchester.

"Listen to this," he said. "It's Debussey's 'Prelude a l'apres-midi d'un faune'. It tells the story of a faun dozing in the reeds, waking briefly to make a play for some nymphs only to sink back into a weary but contented repose." The music was impenetrable, but the more I listened, the more magical and enchanted the esoteric sounds became. "It's like a puzzle, how to appreciate it. It's complex and you need to become familiar with, and to remember each part to enjoy it."

He played it ten times, a mantra that gradually became accessible, even delightful. Single instruments started to conflict then merge, backed by a quiet but full orchestra. They swelled into full strings and horns, and throbbing harps, before retuning to a joyful single state. It was hypnotic, and I found myself falling asleep, dreaming something eminently pleasant, which I couldn't remember when I awoke.

We changed onto the M61 and as we approached the looming city, where poverty mingled with the impressive buildings, sports cars pulled along side us before roaring off in disdain.

"All speed, and no style," dismissed Gatsby.

Finally Gatsby parked the car and then we entered the spacious Foyer of the huge, Victorian Midland Hotel. He pointed out a bronze relief at the entrance. "I like to come here because this is where Charles Stewart Rolls and Frederick Henry Royce used to meet, and it all led to the formation of Rolls-Royce Limited in 1906. My Beauford isn't quite there but, she's as good as." Tall black columns held the ceiling high and we ascended carpeted steps to large couches. Here we had afternoon tea.

"How come you live in the Lakes if you need the city so much?" I asked.

"I need people around me Dan, to distract me, but I live in the Lakes so I can escape, at a moments notice, into solitude. High on the mountains. Where I feel in harmony with the hills around me."

"What about the swimming? Doesn't that give you solitude?"

"It helps, and it keeps me fit, keeps me disciplined as well. But I need to be above it all. When I feel driven out by the crowds, that's when I can reach an intensity, and I can feel that I belong, out of reach, a part of the mountain and its crags."

"Do you have family?" I asked him.

"No, not anymore," he replied. He clearly didn't want to talk about it.

Then I continued, I'm not sure why. "Did you ever want children?"

He paused some time before replying. "Plato thought that people sought immortality through their children. But it doesn't matter how many generations you go on, it will all end. Even the Earth will end. The only eternity we can ever reach is in the moment, "the now". But access to "the now" seems impenetrable, like rock."

"Sorry, I don't understand," I said.

"I'm saying that I don't need children. I try and fulfil my life instead. To be all I need to be."

"A flower is all it needs to be but it still gives rise to new flowers."

"Yes it has its moment of perfection, but the bees still take its pollen and the wind blows its seed. I'm the same, but with ideas. That's how Plato says we get true immortality."

"What, when our ideas live on?" I asked.

"No, when we connect to the eternal Truth, the highest Idea, in the now," said Gatsby. "And when we connect to the perfect 'now', then we can realise that every moment, no matter how mundane, is perfect." His eyes seemed to glaze, then he shook it off as he noticed two ladies enter the hotel. "Anyway, back down to earth. I work with the Johnson-Smythes. I'd like you to meet them. They're famous round here for putting art and antiques in the homes of the wealthy. They have lots of connections with clients in the North, Manchester, Cheshire and around the world. They are art dealers, interior designers."

We met with the dark haired Johnson-Smythes. I was surprised how young the two sisters, Jane and Isobel, looked. Turned out that they had, sadly, inherited their father's business. Then we headed to a warehouse in the Northern Quarter, the creative hub of Manchester just off the city centre. The Johnson-Smythes warehouse was in amongst the narrow streets of old textile buildings. The ground floor was the auction room and the other floors were for viewing the 'collectables.' We entered the huge space.

It was dark, a jumble of antiques in a warren of shelves and clothes rails. Stacks of shoes and books mixed with Victorian furniture and Georgian antiques. I headed to the glass cabinets that were showing off delicate jewellery and ornaments as well as themselves. An old golf set caught my eye, "hickory stick clubs, pre-1935," explained Gatsby.

"Do you have any old croquet sets?" I asked.

"Only table croquet."

I raised an eyebrow and he showed me a battered old box with some small, finely turned mallets and small hoops and balls.

"Have it," suggested the Johnson-Smythes. I thanked them

"People bring items and we get them from house clearance. We select from the best here to put on view in the auction house.

We produce a catalogue and an online catalogue with different special interest auctions," said the Johnson-Smythes.

"I select the antiques to go in my house from here," said Gatsby. "They operate a sale or return. It works well. They find the items, to my specifications, and then deliver them. I advertise them in my rooms and website and then we auction them back here in Manchester."

"How do you protect them from damage?" I asked Gatsby.

"I've got cameras in the antiques rooms, and we never had anyone not pay for any damages."

"So how did you meet Gatsby?" I asked the two ladies.

"We met him after he came back from Afghanistan. He was looking for some trading partners so our father helped him with his art and antiques."

"And how did you get to be interested in antiques?" I asked Gatsby.

"I worked in property and then studied a Masters in Business at Harvard. When I returned to England I carried on in property but also started a business importing and exporting antiques."

"Is that when you met?" I asked.

"No, I joined the Territorial Army, got to the position of Lieutenant and then volunteered to serve in Afghanistan. In the Afghan war I got offered to cut a deal with the Taliban on the opium fields. Reported it and got into all sorts of trouble. But couldn't do that though. Not after what they did to my friends. Killed, or legs and arms blown off, or disfigured, or the damage that you can't see, that's all in here," he touched to his head. "And, because I hadn't compromised in Afghanistan, connections put me in touch with Mr Johnson-Smythe."

I had doubted him until he spoke of his friends.

"But, you know, the most important thing I learned at Harvard was how the directors of big businesses seldom stop and think about the lives they might be destroying with their businesses. They have no regard for the small people. Mr Johnson-Smythe was different, he had a heart. But I don't really mind what I sell to the other business people."

I began to doubt him again. "How come you call yourself Gatsby?"

"I always liked the story by E Scott Fitzgerald, and I wanted to be a part of that lost era. So when Mr Johnson-Smythe told me I was like Gatsby it just stuck."

I guessed to myself that the trauma of war made him to want to live in a different world, an escapism. More the Great Escapist than the Great Gatsby. But there was more to it than that. "So why did you take on the persona of Gatsby as well as his name?"

Noticing that he looked perplexed one of the Johnson-Smythes suggested "Anyway, lets go up to the auction room."

"Yes," replied Gatsby, "I want to answer that Dan, but I want to show you the auction of stock from my last party."

The auction room was full of middle aged men and women on rows of green upholstered chairs. The suited auctioneer presided, with his grey hair and glasses, at a raised table at the far end. Antiques on rows of shelves around the room were also displayed on a big TV screen when it was their turn. The photos were much brighter and clearer than the same actual objects in the room.

"Sold," said the auctioneer. "A fine powder-blue-and-gilt-decorated, Yen-Yen vase. Qing dynasty, Kangxi period."

I was pleasantly surprised to see Dwayne at the front, taking bids from the internet sitting next to a team taking bids on their mobile phones.

"The auction room takes 16%," said Gatsby.

Then lot 367 came up. "A large Qing Dynasty 18th century finely decorated dragon jar with a dragon leaping around a flaming pearl," the auctioneer began, "flanked by four dragons amidst clouds above a band of crashing waves. Neck decorated with four lion heads under a Greek key fret border." He then began to call "At 4,000, 3,500, 3,000, bid, 3,000 bid, 3,500."

A Chinese man held up his a card for bidding, a lady was seated next to him.

"3,500 bid, 3,500, 4,000 for anyone?" After a period of silence he hit his hammer. "Done at 3,500 pounds."

The Chinese couple had won the bowl. And as they got up to walk out I realised, it was Xing and Meihua.

Xing saw Gatsby and froze. It was obvious that he was cheating on Rose, the way he held Meihua. I wondered what was making Gatsby angry, but now know it was because he could see Xing was treating Rose like that.

"Hi Dan," said Xing. "Sorry we can't stay. Hello Mr Gatsby, maybe I can visit you sometime. There is something I'd like to discuss."

"Just pop by, old sport," said Gatsby through his teeth.
And as they left Gatsby turned to me and said, "what an un-mitigated cad."

"A large straw-glazed pottery amphora. Sui-Early Tang dynasty," announced the auctioneer.

Our return journey was more eventful and less pleasurable than the morning drive. On the way back Gatsby's car was smoothly singing, humming and gliding its way up the M6. Debussey's flutes, clarinets, harps and horns, like hunting horns, called out their haunting melody, whose gentle tones, played loud, mixed with the low growl of the engine. I was relaxed, staring out of the window, contemplating, though, that I had never seen a more perfect display of mutual disdain, suppressed for the purpose of potential brinkmanship, than that between Gatsby and Xing.

"Damn, I've got no acceleration," announced Gatsby as he put the left indicator on. We were stuck in the middle lane, cars overtaking in the fast lane and with a white van bearing down onto the back of us, horn blaring.
As we slowed the white van flashed and overtook, its driver raging anger in his face. The lorry to our left undertook, then we flit into the side, swerving onto the hard shoulder, past another lorry behind that sounded it's horn. My heart was pounding as its wheels rolled by. Finally we came to a halt. And we both looked at each other.

"Sorry about that old sport," says Gatsby, "it just goes with the territory of having an old car. I'd prefer if you didn't tell any guests. They might not feel safe to be collected in the old girl."

Gatsby got under the steering wheel.

"Throttle cable snapped, quite an easy job, I just don't carry one with me so I'll have to get breakdown recovery, get them to fetch me one. They just go every five years or so. I'm surprised Dave didn't spot it. He's one of the leading lights of the Lakeland Historic Car Club."

The next evening I sat with Becca on the bench outside my lodge, whilst the sun set. I wanted to ask her about Xing. I knew they were close through her playing poker and Mah Jong for him. She selected a tune from her Ipad list of music from the Roaring 20's.

"This is the Sheik of Araby," she said.

"Gatsby was playing this the other day," I replied.

"Yes, he played it to me as well. Kind of grows on you doesn't it."

"He said it was all about how a Sheikh kidnaps a woman, whisks her away until she falls in love with him."

"Xing did that with Rose in Shanghai. And now Gatsby wants to do the same, wants to captivate her with his charm. Ha, ha."

"What do you mean?" I asked.

"Gatsby told me that he used to be in love with Rose, before he went to Afghanistan. The thought of seeing her again kept him going through the conflict. They used to go out in Manchester, ballroom dancing. And then, when he announced that he was leaving to serve in Helmund Province, she found someone else. It broke his heart. But he believed that she loved him. She just hadn't told him because he had never been able to tell her that he loved her. He was too embarrassed. So he never had closure. He believes that she threw him over because she was angry."

"Anyway, her new love didn't last and she went to China, to study Chinese at Shanghai University. That's where she met Xing. They had a whirlwind romance and a beautiful wedding, I was her bridesmaid. She wore a red bridal gown. It was stunning. And everything was perfect for her until the scandal. When Xing had an accident in his Ferrari and another girl was in the car. She was in a coma for weeks. She survived, but for the son of a Chinese Official to be involved, it was a disgrace. He had to leave and so they came to Britain to live. They mixed with a fast set who drink too much, spend too much, gamble and take stuff. But Rose didn't take it."

"So now he's in the Lakes, and Gatsby is Rose's next door neighbour. Does she know?"

"No, but I think he moved to the Lakes to be near her. He thought that she might have come to one of his parties, but she isn't into all this vintage and her partying days are over. That's why she came up to the Lakes, to get away from those crowds."

"Why didn't he just Facebook friend her or something?"

"He looked her up online but didn't want to friend her as her profile is private. And he knew that she's married now, so he didn't want to interfere."

"Well," I said, "he knows now that Xing has been cheating on her."

"Yes and that's why he wants to meet Rose at your place."

"Does Rose want to see Gatsby?" I asked.

"It's hard to say. I told Rose about Gatsby's parties, and showed her a photo from Hello magazine. She seemed to recognise him and wanted to know who he was but wouldn't tell me why. All I know is that Gatsby told me a romantic story, and told me that she knows him by another name, Jim Baxter."

"Well does she want to see whoever he is?"

"She's not to know about it. It's to be a surprise."

"I don't think I can do that," I replied.

"You know how much Xing cheats on her. Just do something for her for once won't you."

"I, I…"

"Look, just invite Rose over to your lodge, to paint her. That will get her to come," said Becca.

"She'll just want me to go over to her house."

"Just insist, for artistic reasons," she put her hand on my thigh. "Besides, I feel awkward showing her your painting of me until after you've done one of her."

I kissed Becca as the sun set over the Lakeland hills.

Chapter 5

MY RURAL SENSIBILITY returned and I was back in tweed and jeans, dictated to by weather that was distinctly chillier. The rain hammered down, day after day, and my little lodge began to feel like a bit of a prison, or a monastic cell. I was either now relaxing or starting to get bored. And I hadn't determined which. So I finally conceded and invited Rose to tea and so that I could start painting her portrait. And I told her to come alone, as instructed. My easel and canvas were set up, waiting for my guests. I would work from life, no photos and I would paint in oils.

The rain had stopped when Gatsby arrived in his three-piece tweed suit, with matching cap. He looked every inch a country gentleman. He brought just one pink rose.

"That's not a very Gatsby way to do things," I said.

"I'm a Modern Gatsby."

"Postmodern actually," I remarked.

"Look, I can't do it like in the book," he said. "Too many flowers, it just wouldn't be appropriate."

He was referring to the eponymous book. We were playing out a scene from The Great Gatsby, only in a new and exciting way. I was interested to see how it would all evolve. I just hoped that Rose wouldn't mind.

Gatsby sniffed the air in disapproval. "Do you think we could open a couple of windows. And can we have a cloth on the table as well."

"I don't have one."

"I'll go and get one, I didn't realise it was like this." Gatsby looked at my jeans. "And sorry old sport, I want things to be just right."

I shook my head.

"I bet you think I'm being dramatic," said Gatsby.

"I wouldn't expect any less from you," I replied as I went to change my jeans and he went to get the table cloth.

Gatsby returned just as it started to rain. I flicked the kettle on as my mobile rang. "It's Rose." I put my finger to my lips. "She's here and she wants me to bring an umbrella to the car."

"Where should I wait?" asked Gatsby. "In the other room?"

I nodded and I grabbed an umbrella and headed down the steps.

"I feel an idiot. I shouldn't have done this."

I could see his chest heaving, almost hear his heart beating.

Rose was sitting, looking forlorn in a small BMW sports car. She was heavily made up, and her hair was over curled. I held the umbrella over her as she got out. "I'm going to have to do all this again," she tutted.

I'd asked her to wear something simple, to make it easier to paint her, so she wore a plain white dress. "Do you have a coat?" I asked as she shivered.

"Yes, I brought a fur. I want you to make me look glamorous and devastating."

I took Rose up the steps to the lodge where she immediately headed for the bedroom.

"Don't go in there," I ordered.

"Why not, don't be ashamed. I've seen worse."

To my relief Gatsby wasn't in there. She found the mirror in my bedroom and arranged her hair before coming into the lounge to sit in the chair, my easel and paints in front of her.

"You're right. I don't mean to be funny, but how can you live here Dan," she asked, "it's so basic. Okay for a holiday, but not to live here. Oh and the tartan curtains are too interesting. We really must tell Xing to do something about them"

I laughed, "Shame you hadn't seen the room before I moved in. You get used to it. In fact I think I'm quite fond of the curtains now. Anyway I'll just bring the kettle back to the boil and make a pot of tea."

There was a heavy clatter on the roof. A grand finale and then the weather appeared to be clearing up so I opened the French window doors. Looking out from the lodge the patter of rain became a gentle rustle on the canopy of trees, ebbing and flowing, surging, sighing.

"Why did you ask me to come alone?" asked Rose.

"It spoils the artistic concentration to have an audience." I replied. "That said, I have a visitor who said he wanted to see you."

"I'm intrigued."

Gatsby came in, wet, with three more pink roses. "I just got some more roses. I chose them for their scent. It's divine. Really citrussy."

Rose was surprised to see him but showed that she was pleased, giving him that look of sharing happiness. "Hello Jim," she said.

"I was drenched in seconds," he added.

Rose was nervous as the refreshing wet petals touched her nose as she breathed in deeply. "Wow, that's beautiful."

I watched Gatsby's face as he processed his reaction to Rose. He looked like he felt that she wasn't as beautiful as he remembered her, that she had aged. Then he re-saw her, with a gentle tenderness that recognises the mortality of beauty. As if he was looking at a matured flower in a vase, just as beautiful, only in a different way, maybe fuller and perfected. "Hello Rose," he finally said.

"You look very warm. Aren't you going to take off your cap and jacket?" asked Rose.

"Don't you like them?" replied Gatsby. "They're Harris Tweed."

"No they look, I mean you look, splendid," she reassured.

He took them off and sat in his tweed waistcoat, still the epitome of style. He began to look at her, as if he was gazing at the night sky, marvelling at the stars and constellations.

I got up and made the tea. I spent longer than I needed to arranging the tray, the teapot, the cups and saucers, the sugar, the milk jug, some plates and some biscuits. "I'm afraid it's not quite Chinese Tea," I said to Rose as I finally put the tray onto the table.

"What a coincidence, that you live across from us," said Rose. "And that you came by to Dan's today. Are you going to be staying long?"

"Yes, maybe permanently, or at least until I've done what I set out to do."

"No, I mean this afternoon. Dan says that an audience spoils his concentration."

Gatsby stared at me like, for once, he didn't actually know what to do. He reached no conclusion. Just clicked into automatic, asking Rose, "Do you have children?"

"Yes. A boy."

"How is your husband?"

"He's fine, and what are you up to these days?"

"Oh, various things. I'm into investments, property, shares, antiques, things like that. And I put on events, all sorts really."

They both seemed awkward and embarrassed.

I poured the tea and asked how they liked it, then thought of an excuse to leave. "Oh, I've forgotten my turps. It must be in the car."

"I'll go. Just give me the key," requested Gatsby.

"No, its okay, I know where it is."

"Just tell me where it is."

"No, you both stay and have a cup of tea," I insisted. "I won't be a moment."

It was raining again. So when I got to my car I sat there like Descartes in his oven. Keeping warm and dry. 'Cogito Ergo Sum', 'I think therefore I am.' What is it to be someone these days. Who was this Jim person anyway. What was I dreaming of leaving them there together. How long should I wait. Then the phone rang. It was Rose.

"Have you got it yet?"

"Emm, it wasn't where I thought it was. I just got it now." ·

When I returned Rose was alone.

"Where's Gatsby?" I enquired.

"He had to get back to his house. To prepare it for our visiting him later. Funny, seeing him again. We used to dance together. What a remarkable coincidence you living next door to him in Xing's lodges."

"Yes," I replied, though I was beginning to doubt the coincidence.

"He insisted I go to see his house Dan. You'll go with me though won't you. After you've painted me of course." She smiled winsomely.

"I'll do the preliminary sketch and put a base coat of paint down and then we can go and have a look."

"I guess it will be a good break," said Rose.

The rain stopped and I dried the bench outside my French windows. I sat Rose there then sketched her, from the waist up, and the scene behind her. There was something hard in her face. Almost from disdain at all the tiresome suitors who had sought to win her over. Rose was getting cold and tired already. I started to regret agreeing to do the painting. I painted the sky, the mountains and the lake in light shades, then added the jetty and a couple of boats. With stronger, darker browns and greens I added the trunks of the trees, the branches and leaves. I was building it up, layer by layer. Next came the undercoat for Rose's dress and fur. "It'll be a nice break to visit Gatsby's," I suggested.

The sun was out by the time we made our way through the woods over to meet Gatsby at the front of the house. A mason sat on top of scaffolding at the side of the porch, chiselling away at the corner of one of the lotus buds on the entablature.

"This is my ancestral home," said Gatsby. "Only I'm the beginning of the line."

"How did you manage to afford all this?" asked Rose.

"Various business ventures. Like I said, I work in property, shares, events, as well as antiques and vintage. I'm a middleman. And it's always the middleman who makes the money. But the building still needs work. It's a restoration project. I'll do it up, then onto the next thing. It's stuccoed sandstone ashlar." As he explained he looked at Rose, not me, I could see how he was trying his hardest to impress.

We entered the mansion where we were met with the snarling head a very old white tiger rug. On the walls were the heads of deer, stags, antelopes, foxes and pheasants. They looked on with glazed eyes, like the blank staring CCTV cameras above the doors. Stuffed animals added to the menagerie. They stood, caged behind glass sharing the corners with leafy plants.

We passed over a Persian rug into a room that stretched from the front of the house to the back with a doorway between the two sections. All the doors were mahogany, with ebony beading and strips of brass inlay. Around them were heavy white frames. A luxurious cornice, with acanthus leaves and scrolls, ran around the room. Below this ran a frieze with alternating vine leaves and bunches of grapes. Heavy tasselled curtains hung by thick poles with leaf bladed ends.

Tall pink and purple orchids sat on small side tables and the room was full of table lamps. I realised, when I counted the lamps and the bulbs in a glass chandelier, that it must've used less energy to burn all the lamps than a single Chandelier.

A delicate eighteenth century print in a gilded frame caught Rose's eye. "I've got all sorts of Lakeland prints and paintings," explained Gatsby. "Like these by William Payne and William Green and photographs by the Abraham brothers and early Heaton Cooper paintings."

Rose couldn't help herself as she adopted a mocking English phrasing. "Oh, how awfully nice. Simply spiffing."

A grandfather clock chimed. A minute later another, further in the room, rang out, out of unison. Gatsby pulled the chains on the grandfather clocks. Their ticking was restful, with solid, deep tones. Presiding over the smaller clocks that sat quietly on delightful marble mantelpieces, besides which stood china vases.

"I mean, I don't want to sound a little stupid, but why not just get new things?" asked Rose mischievously.

"It's the quality, you just can't get it any more. Everything's from China, just badly made and with cheap materials."

Rose's face dropped at the comment, "I know what you mean, but the quality is getting better all the time."

An arched opening led to a central rotunda. We entered this round room directly under the beautiful dome and the balustrades of the first floor gallery. This circular hall was lit by the dome above and had four arched entrances. "These go to the dining room, the lounge and to the staircase," said Gatsby. In four alcoves sat white busts of Roman Gods, most notable of which Pan, playing his pipes. He had small horns, pointed ears and small beard.

We headed to the stairway where a tapestry of knights in Italian landscapes and cityscapes hung.

The cantilevered staircase, with decorative brass balustrade, turned sharp right angles and took us onto the round balcony that looked down to the white busts of gods below. The dome, whose glass was light blue, orange, and yellow, had ribs to a floral roundel. It was like a pagan heaven. Not in cold white, but where colours dappled the walls.

Gatsby's bedroom had a four poster bed, on which lay a big white heart-shaped box of chocolates. The room commanded views out over the lake. We admired the long, splendid view down the length of Windermere and then Gatsby took the chocolates and offered Rose one. 'Handmade from Belgium.' They were all there.

"I couldn't."

"No please. Look," Gatsby took one and popped it in his mouth.

So she took one, realising it would be rude not to.

I held my hand up to decline, so that Gatsby didn't feel he needed to offer me. He didn't and put them down, as if having made progress with Rose. Then he went to an old burr walnut wardrobe and pulled out an extendable chrome hanging rail. "Here are some of my jackets and suits." I admired how the wardrobes had original labels from the 1920s. 'collars', 'ties', 'pyjamas.' He opened his tallboy and pulled out the drawers "And my fine shirts, and ties originals from America, or London, Saville Row. It's almost all vintage. I get it off my dealers or off the internet. You can't get this quality any more. Shirts these days just don't cut the mustard. Look." He opened the drawers and took out small bakelite boxes full of exquisite tie-pins, cufflinks, collar studs and rings. "You can't find anything new like this."

Rose went over to his deco vanity unit and sat in front of the round mirror. She smelled some of Gatsby's fragrances and then started to cry.

"What's wrong?" asked Gatsby.

"It's such a shame," she sighed, laughing at herself. "All this beauty, all this quality. It's all disappearing. All going."

"High in a white palace, the king's daughter, the golden girl," said Gatsby, smiling.

She smiled back. Then Gatsby opened an art deco desk and turned on the chrome laptop inside. "I've got a photo to show you." And whilst he searched the internet I looked at the photographs on the wall of Gatsby with a group of soldiers in Afghanistan, and a photo of him with his Beauford, looking like Robert Redford. Most striking of all was a photo of him aged eighteen years old, smiling, happier than I had seen him, with a soldier I assumed to be his brother.

"Look, here's a photo of us when we used to dance together," he said. "A lady e-mailed it to me years ago."

They both looked happy, laughing, gazing each others' eyes. Now his expression was deep.

"Oh my God, I didn't realise you had that photo. Ha, I look awful."

"No, you look beautiful."

She blushed.

We moved lazily, down into the dining room where Gatsby insisted on sitting Rose in prime position. And we looked out of the window, at the elegant gardens running down to the lake.

Dwayne brought tea, coffee and homemade shortbread thins, in the shape of flowers, on a silver tray. There was cream for coffee and milk for tea. Gatsby poured and shared the plate of biscuits. The unsalted butter thins soon crumbled in the mouth.

"I'll put on some records," he said, bringing out a wind-up gramophone. He inserted the arm and wound it up. The old shellac 78 spun.

'You're the cream in my coffee,
you're the salt in my stew,

you will always be my necessity,
I'd be lost without you.

You're the starch in my collar,
you're the lace in my shoe,
you will always be my necessity,
I'd be lost without you.'

We all tapped our toes and as the music played it drew up a response from Rose that was almost atavistic, reverting her to anachronistic Englishness.

"Oh, how delightful. Simply divine."

Then Gatsby's phone rang and he lifted the needle arm from the record. "Sorry." He answered the phone. "Yes, send us up the usual amount, we've got a few hundred guests. Some of them big buyers." At that he got up and went to the bar. He put three glasses down.

"Would you like Champagne?" he asked Rose.

"No thanks," she replied, no longer captivated. He opened the bottle anyway.

"It's vintage."

"Alright, a tiny sip. Thanks."

He brought the glasses over but it seemed as thought the only thing sweetening the silence was the taste of the Champagne.

Gatsby lit a cigarette from an old silver case. His hand was shaking. Rose coughed and he put it out straight away.

"No please, don't on my account."

"No, I don't, just occasionally, when I'm a bit nervous. And now I've got smoke all in the room. How dashed inconsiderate. Let's go outside."

And so we wandered around the gardens, past the croquet lawn, past the pinks, mauves and blues of the hydrangeas and down to the lake side. "Oh, how beautiful, little Singapore orchids," said Rose as we walked through the grounds.

We had made a circuit of the gardens and arrived back near the front of the house. We didn't go into the woods and Gatsby told Rose he would save the Temple for another day. He pointed across the water to her house. "See how close you are. You don't need to drive all the way around." Then he pointed down to the jetty. "You can moor a boat here, it's so easy to visit, if you want to."

And then we were back at the entrance porch.

"Well, thank you Jim. I think we need to go now. Dan has a painting of me to do."

"I wouldn't want to get in the way of that," he replied. "I'd love to be able to paint you. To capture your beauty."

She blushed.

In return Gatsby breathed triumphantly, she had seen him again and now she knew how he felt.

Rose looked at me like it was all too much. "We better go." She turned back to Gatsby. "It was nice to bump into you."

"Yes, I will look forward to seeing you again." It was the second time she blushed, embarrassed, unnerved. Gatsby picked up on this. "I mean in Dan's painting of you."

"Yes," she smiled and gave him a warm look.

After we came back from Gatsby's I was able to reflect on my painting. It always pays to take some time away from your work, helps you to be more critical. It was starting to look sharp and angular. So I paid attention to smoothing the lines as I began working on some more of the detail. I had to get it right this time, not like my humble effort to capture Becca. So I had to compromise. I took a photograph of Rose before the blanket of cloud returned and brought a faint drizzle with it.

We stopped for the day and I steadfastly refused to show it to her. She would have to wait until it was finished.

Chapter 6

THE REPUTATION OF Gatsby's parties and auctions spread. He was now the subject of press attention. Blogs and Facebook sites promoted him and only the exclusive could get tickets to his parties. Yet no one knew who he really was. We assumed that the mystery was all a theatrical device, a publicity stunt. Then one afternoon, when I had just sent Gatsby's ball into the hydrangeas with a particularly mean croquet shot, instead of calling him Gatsby as he retrieved his ball from the undergrowth I said, "Sorry about that Jim". It was a bit like a flood barrier breaking.

"Dan, I'd like to talk, to be honest, I need someone to talk to about things." We sat on one of the ironwork benches. "You know, my real name is Jim, James, Baxter. I'd like to share a bit about myself. I was born in Manchester. And my mother was a single parent. We had little money and lived in a council house. I spent as much time out of school as in it and was told I'd never get any qualifications. My mother didn't care for my education much, or for me and my brother for that matter. She had an accidental drugs overdose, she needed help but ended up taking too many sleeping pills. I was bright and landed myself a job in property early on and built up a portfolio of bigger and better houses. I had a talent at selling, and was told that my smile charmed everyone I met. I earned enough money in property to get an education. Did so well I ended up going to Harvard Business School"

"But I never really had girlfriends," he continued. "I'm confident in business, but not with women. I have nothing to talk about with them. So I built up a persona until I knew that they liked me. I built up my skill in ballroom dancing to meet a girl with some class."

"Yes, but all you talk about is what you are interested in, not what they are interested in."

"You're right, of course, but I get obsessed, and that's because I'm a visionary and I want perfection that I was too self-absorbed and too shy. I had some relationships but they were too hollow. It was love that I needed. Love and beauty. Beauty inside. That is what I needed most. I took up ballroom dancing. I loved the romance of it. Thought I'd meet someone graceful, inside," he put his hand to his heart. "I would've gone further with dancing. Then my older brother was killed in Iraq. He'd been a soldier for ten years. Blown up by an I.E.D." I remembered the photo of a young Gatsby next to a soldier.

"I don't know why, but I thought I could change things so I joined the Territorial Army and volunteered to serve in Afghanistan. It was there that I realised that the real war was in economics. So when I returned I grew my businesses." I felt privileged that he had confided in me but before he went any further he headed from the lawn. "I can hear someone coming," he said. I couldn't hear anything, I just followed.

At the front of his mansion a red Ferrari and two BMW roadsters pulled up. Xing got out of the Ferrari but his friends, a Chinese man and woman, stayed in their roadsters.

"Hello old sport," says Gatsby

Xing laughed and replied, "Ni hao laoshi yundong."

"What's that mean."

"The same, only in Mandarin."

"To what do I owe the pleasure?" asked Gatsby.

"You don't owe me anything. We are on a little road race. We thought we'd go to Ambleside, then up to Kirkstone Pass and down into Patterdale and round Keswick, Grasmere and back to Windermere. But we need something to stimulate us. Adds to the excitement." Xing put a finger under his nose and sniffed.

"I don't advise taking anything and driving."

"Oh, it's for later," Xing laughed. But Gatsby recognised it was a feigned gesture of assurance.

"I don't have anything like that."

Xing stared at him, "I thought you supplied all your guests' needs," then turned and laughed, "We don't need anything anyway, they are such great roads around here. Why don't you come on the drive, you could bring Dan?"

"What, in the Beauford. I don't think she's up to it, not got the road holding. And she's not fast enough. She does alright on the motorway but I don't have the same acceleration."

"What about in your BMW, or Dan's car?"

"To be honest, my racing days are over. I'm not interested in competing over anything anymore. I'm more interested in being graceful, not frantic."

"What are you into competing over? There must be something."

Gatsby blushed. Did Xing know of his interest in Rose. What had Rose said.

"I just do what I do. And if it works then great. If it makes me money, even better. However, I am interested in exporting to China. Maybe you can help?"

"Maybe," said Xing. "First we need to build some Guanxi. We should talk about it at one of your parties. I'll bring some friends over. Let them amuse themselves and we can discuss it over some fine cigars."

"Splendid, a most agreeable idea. You could bring some of your croupiers for my gaming table."

"Yes, splendid, as you would say. And maybe we can make it a 1920's Shanghai themed night."

Gatsby's eyes lit. "Yes, maybe. I'll ask the Johnson-Smythes to bring some extra Oriental antiques."

"Oh, I meant to tell you," said Xing. "You looked lost on the water the other day. I came out from my house to show you where to land. I saw you were bobbing about, out of control. I thought you were going to visit then I wondered if I needed to call for the lake warden to help you."

"Thanks," said Gatsby. "I think we decided it was too wet."

"Well, we'll see you soon," said Xing as he returned to his car.

We waved, to be civil, then when they had driven away Gatsby turned to me "Some people just have to try and spoil a perfect day."

"I thought he was just telling us that he'd been trying to be helpful," I suggested.

"No, he could see we were having fun, and got jealous. But it's fine. He's just a mere ripple on the water."

Midsummer had just passed and this was the hottest, driest day of the summer. The party that evening was hot. Chinese lanterns hung from trees. And flags and bunting flew down the length of the lawn. Out on the lawn my hands were clammy, eyes squinting, skin feeling tight on my face and loose on my body. Everyone had less on than usual. Ladies' backs, red from too much sun, merged and contrasted with their Oriental parasols. Their beautiful dresses adapted for the weather.

The men wore Mandarin collar jackets, naval uniforms, boating blazers or dinner jackets, but bow ties soon disappeared along with all pretence of upper class civility. It was easy to see the party, and the people at it, for what it was. An exercise in hedonism and narcissism. The Lake Windermere had become one giant pool of Narcissus. The guest staring in love at their own reflections of glamorous partying.

Mr Rajaratnam and Mr Mukherjee, in Mandarin collar jackets and sandals, were doing their best to follow the teachers of Tai Chi on the lawn. A jazz band, complete with xylophone, played Chinese influenced, Shanghai jazz, under a real Pagoda. The "Chinese Charleston" by Honey Duke was being sung by the thin Jazz singer in round glasses as he played the ukelele:

'Underneath the Jack-o-lantern rays,
Jazz band play the latest craze.
China Town it used to be so dreary,
Now is gay and oh so cheery,
Every little boy and girl Chinese
Shake their crazy knees.
Xing Ling Po he learn to do the Charleston, Charleston,
You should see the Chinese do the Charleston, Charleston.
Everything is upside down,
Down in dreamy China Town,
He taught them all to do the Chinese Charleston,
Charleston.'

Down at the lakeside people were playing with swans, feeding them or photographing them. Two swans bent for food. Their necks arched at the same time, making the shape of a heart, as RAF fighter jets silently covered the long approach. They flew low then passed with a roar that ripped into the air. It created a stir amongst the guests, whose attention focussed to one place for the first time, decimating the background quiet and leaving the raucous noise of the guests in the shade.

Watching over the scene was Gatsby. Who, despite the heat, presided in sartorial splendour. He wore a white felt hat, a white suit and shirt, with a black tie, black breast pocket handkerchief and black and white wingtip shoes. He was pleased that I noticed the gold collar pin holding his tie in place. I joined him as two ladies did a drunken tango the length of the terrace.

"That looks like fun," I said.

"At the parties," replied Gatsby, "I do my best to encourage people to dance the Charleston, Tango, Waltz and Foxtrot."

There was a small group doing these dances, but it was too hot and the majority preferred to watch or just staggered around. A large group had gathered around a girl dancing on a table.

A yacht sailed past the front of the house. Its two white sails reflected in the still water. A red dragon flag flew from the mast. "Its Rose and Becca," I said. We watched as other boats swerved, with near misses, to avoid the straight line he had plotted.

"Let's follow it," suggested Gatsby. So we walked through the wood, following the boat, past the temple and to the jetty where they came to rest.

Xing jumped onto the jetty and tied up the yacht. He wore shorts and trainers, contrasting with his bow tie and dinner jacket. He had gold rimmed sunglasses on the rim of his Panama hat. Rose and Becca stepped onto the jetty. They wore the tradition Shanghai qipao.

Gatsby seemed embarrassed at Xing's presence but still took us around, introducing us to various celebrities and influential business people. The guests were all commenting on how great it was that Gatsby kept things fresh and new. But it seemed like less of the aristocratic and respected guests were present. It was more of the hangers on and the lowest common denominator.

Dwayne came out with Champagne in an ice bucket on a silver tray. We all took a glass, and called "Gan Bei!" We drank, but Rose sipped.

"Liao bu qi de gai ci bi zai fang," said Xing.

Rose and Becca laughed.

"And in English?" Gatsby asked.

"Great Gatsby Revisited," said Xing. "We see you again."

"Indeed. Here's to a great Shanghai Night."

"Gan Bei!" I added.

"So about the business proposition that I wanted to ask you about," said Gatsby.

"Yes?" replied Xing. Gatsby led us onto the terrace.

"I want to sell antiques in China."

"You mean your junk and second hand?"

"No, high quality."

Xing laughed. "You British sold most of it to the Americans already."

"We've still got plenty of good items. But the American market has dried up. Anyway, you import container loads of Chinese reproductions, so why not export some container loads of originals. It's better than sending back empty containers."

"Oh, like asset stripping? Your thinking is too small. I've been thinking about this a lot lately. We have a lot of Chinese people moving here. So if we sell British antiques in China then we won't be able to sell the English country houses to the Chinese, as we won't have anything left to put in them. Besides, the value of the pound has still got a way to fall against the Yuan. So I'll wait for it to drop further. And when it does your antiques will be cheaper for us. That's when we'll start selling to the Chinese people online on Taobao."

"Well, I also sell property," said Gatsby, "so maybe we can work together, selling refurbished country houses."

"Ha, ha, you are my competitor, and I'm winning."

"The East may have taken on Western business skills," replied Gatsby, "but the West has taken on Eastern wisdom."

The conversation was interrupted by a gong being beaten to announce that dinner was served. In the dining room we helped ourselves to the Chinese buffet then took our seats back on the terrace. I succeeded in eating my tofu with chopsticks and was dismayed to see Xing using a fork. The weather was so hot that the guests didn't want much and lots was left to waste. Then a young lady dressed as a coolie took a photo of me with chopsticks.

"How do you feel about people taking photos and filming the whole evening and putting it on Facebook and Youtube?" I asked Gatsby.

"I'm not sure," said Gatsby, "I thought it was good publicity. And it is when people want to be seen with the 'right' people. But we may have started to attract a few bounders and such so it may be putting people off. Personally speaking, I think snapshots are okay, but I don't see the point of making life about photographing life, rather than living it. I like to honour the experience for what it is, at the time. Not make it something for future review."

I was wondering how that squared with living life through a role, a fictional persona when Meihua and some other of Xing's Casino staff came to our table. I noticed how Xing took pleasure in her attention and the discomfort of Rose. It was clear that Meihua was at the party, by Xing's arrangement, and that he was all but actually accompanying her.

"Ni hao Dan," said Meihua. "I'm so excited to be here. Isn't it just great."

"Yes, great." I now felt completely complicit in the insult being caused to Rose. I only hoped that Gatsby could restore some of her dignity. Remove some of the shame that should fall to Xing, but that he was putting onto her.

"Xing, I need some help with the blackjack table," said Meihua.

The moon had risen Rose held Xing with a fixed gaze, needy of approval. "Wo hen ai ta," she said. Whatever the words were, it was obvious what they meant.

"I know that you love me," said Xing, pretending to be unclear why she had told him. "My father asked me to entertain some of his clients. So I've invited them to our gaming table tonight. They are important merchants, gold from South Africa, oil from Nigeria, diamonds from Namibia and coffee from Kenya. They are here and I need to look after them."

"Don't you want to introduce me?" asked Rose.

"No, it's gaming, you know I want to keep you out of that side of the business. I won't be long, just enjoy the party," said Xing as he disappeared with Meihua.

Gatsby sympathised at her hurt, his gaze lingered, betraying his own love. But Rose didn't notice it. "Why don't we all go to the Temple," he said. "I told you I was going to show it you."

"Yes, it's great," I emphasised, taking Rose by the arm, taking her away from her thoughts.

I headed with Gatsby, Rose and Becca down to the Lakeside, to the path into the wood. The air felt close and thick black clouds were beginning to move in from the south west. They were heading towards the blue moon. A moth crashed against a Chinese lantern hanging from a tree.

Becca whispered to my ear. "Don't you think that Gatsby, like so many people here, is like a moth around a flame." Then she said out loud, "I have to go and teach people how to play Mah Jong," she slipped away, walking backwards, "my job for the night, unfortunately."

Gatsby switched on the torch on his mobile phone and lit the path into the undergrowth. I didn't think I should follow them, instead I caught up with Becca and headed back to the terrace where she left me to the small groups who competed for attention in loud voices, asserting themselves, their money and who they knew; famous people, bankers, aristocrats.

Rose came out of the undergrowth alone. A short time after Gatsby emerged then stood by the Chinese lantern. I got up and came down the steps between the horses' heads to meet Rose as she crossed the lawns.

"Dan, darling," she said. "Jim took me to his extraordinary little Temple. He asked to dance for old time's sake." I imagined them gliding gently over the cool slate floor. Overlooking the moonlit lake. "But I found it far too scary. So I've come back to find Xing." We went inside and by the time I'd got to the white busts in the rotunda Rose had disappeared in search of Xing. I grabbed a coffee and wondered how I should occupy my time.

Many of the new antiques on display were from the Ming and Qing dynasties. There were carvings of gods and lions in ivory and dogs in jade, beautiful vases, tea sets and bowls. But the rooms were too busy to study them. So I retired to the hallway, and stepped around the white tiger rug, to find a small couch, under a stag's head, next to a palm plant and away from the rutting egos and inappropriately loud voices. I rested with my coffee and then a group came in, drinking cocktails and champagne. Talking about themselves and how frightfully great they were.

I tried to ignore them until one came back announcing "fireworks." So we all headed outside, where fire-crackers jumped, exploding on the terrace and rockets burst into the cloudy sky. They had been lit prematurely, to beat the onset of a storm. They exploded in brilliant patterns and then merged with lightning flashes and thunder. Then they fizzled as it started to rain. It was that really nice, warm summer rain, then it turned into a torrent.

Back inside, Rose stood in the rotunda with Xing, powder under his nose, his eyes wide open. "Gatsby knows how to throw a party, but all this was my idea. A take-over for the evening. It won't be long before we have the parties at our place Rose. Ha, How dya like that?" She looked like she could burst into tears. He knew it and pressed. "Great isn't it."

"Let's go," said Rose.

"You go, I'm just starting to enjoy myself."

"But I want 'us' to go." Her contracted lips and thrusting eyes declared an ultimatum.

"Well, I would go, but I have to look after the tables. You know I said I need to work. I'll be back as soon as I can. Dan will take you. Won't you Dan? I'll tell Becca."

"Sure," I said then turned to Rose, "I'll find Gatsby to let him know."

"No, I'd rather just go. I'm tired and I don't have anything in common with anyone here," said Rose. She seemed almost at the point of breakdown.

Xing went back into the lounge and I supported Rose as we headed for the main entrance. Gatsby must have spotted us, heard us.

"I saw you from the balcony. I've been looking all over for you."

"I'm going."

"What about another dance?"

"No thanks."

"Okay, but let me take you home."

"No, its very kind but Dan's taking me. I need to talk to him about something."

"Well, at least let my chauffeur take you both."

"You need him for your other guests," she replied.

"Then, before you go, at least let me show you some of my new pieces," said Gatsby. "There aren't that many, however, quality is always better than quantity. Look, here's a rare 'Longquan' Celadon 'Bamboo-Neck' Vase, Southern Song Dynasty. And here, a pair of fine and rare 18th century Bajixiang dishes. Look at the scrolling lotus pattern and the band of the Buddhist symbols in red enamel. And on the back, bright pomegranates, peaches and flowers with a Qianlong seal mark."

Rose was backing away to the door, she looked harried, then turned, stumbled on the white tiger rug and knocked over a Chinese vase that contained pink and yellow roses. The vase smashed into large pieces with a dull thud. I bent down to appreciate what was lost. The flowers were gorgeous amongst the sharp shards of beautiful pottery. Fresh and really nice smelling and I felt guilty that I had only noticed them and the vase when they had become detritus.

"I'm sorry," she cried.

"It doesn't matter. It was my fault. I don't normally put them out at parties. I knew you coming so I put them there."

We moved out of the door and to the porch.

"Please, let my chauffeur take you both."

"Alright, alright," she replied, sobbing.

Gatsby called his chauffeur and then held an umbrella over Rose as we went to the car. The chauffeur doffed his cap and opened the door. We got in.

And so I went with Rose from the mansion. The cameras turned to watch as the main gates slowly opened. And as we pulled out of the drive I started to imagine how Gatsby might have felt, dancing with Rose. The smoothness of the movement, the timeless flow. The existing in the perfection. The timeless perfection in beauty, in the mountains and in the lake. As if this was what everything was designed to be, what it should be. Only something bad was in its way, making life ugly, painful, difficult. Only in glimpses and fleeting moments have I partaken of the perfection that we all feel is rightfully ours. But Gatsby was convinced that he had found perfection in Rose. Maybe the dance gave him an illusion that he had reached her inner perfection, in a shared moment. But when they had come from the wood he had stood confused. At that moment, when he danced, his dream had become his greatest reality. In a perfection that was really just a dream. In a moment that couldn't last forever.

I held Rose's hand, but she was silent all the way back to her house. A silence drowned out by the rain.

Chapter 7

GATSBY'S PLACE WAS closed. Maybe it was the rain, maybe it was the economy. Either way, the only signs of life were the rabbits and squirrels bounding over the side lawns. So when I saw Gatsby comes out of the Lake one morning, in his wool swimming costume. I ran through the wood and climbed a fence into his grounds. I met him as he was drying off.

"What ho Gatsby! Why's it so quiet round here now? Is everything alright?"

"It's fine. After Rose came over it was a bit of a turning point for me. I kind of lost the point of throwing parties. I don't really want any at the moment. We've been getting too many of the hoi polloi lately. The riff raff. They just don't get it, and they don't buy. I decided to quit whilst I'm ahead. So I'm downsizing. I've even had to let Dwayne go."

I was surprised, and worried. So when Rose phoned me to meet up with Becca and go to Manchester. I agreed, but I insisted on bringing Gatsby. I didn't like to see him like this, and thought it would do him good. It would do them all good. But apparently he was already coming. Xing had already arranged it. They were to do business, at the Casino and in Gatsby's warehouse. I wondered if it was a genuine business proposition or if Xing just had another call from Meihua to go to China Town.

The weather changed and now the heat was sweltering. Gatsby was still well turned out as we went to Xing and Rose's place. He wouldn't go in my car and said, "I'd struggle to get the Beauford down those roads." So we turned up in Gatsby's wooden motor boat. I was carrying my painting of Rose under my arm. Gatsby had wanted to see it before we got there, but I kept avoiding the matter.

We rang the bell of the Elizabethan style house. Rose greeted us and showed us into the hall. A small boy came around the corner. He was shy, yet haughty. "This is Hu," said Rose, "his name means Tiger. Say hello to our guests." The boy hid his face into his mother's side. He was dressed in a traditional Mandarin style Chinese collar jacket, but with its arms cut off. His hair was slicked back and he wore shorts. "Uncle Dan here has done a painting of mama, would you like to see it?" The boy nodded and then they both took us into the lounge where Xing and Becca were waiting,

A place had been cleared on the mantelpiece for the painting. I unveiled it carefully. It was a perfect photographic likeness, with expressive brush strokes that contoured the lines of Rose's face and body. It was a good work, that had met with Rose's approval, but I was disappointed that I had done it from a photograph.

Xing paid for the painting, almost resentfully, saying how he intended to get a fashionable Chinese artist to paint both of them at some future time. We drank Chinese green tea in small cups. Then a jet ripped through the air and the black poodle started barking.

We went into the garden, by the lake, under the shade of trees and paddled in the cooling water. Xing's boat stood proud.

"You should paint this scene," suggested Rose.

"The light is difficult," I replied, "makes it hard to make the water and sky look real."

"You live over there don't you?"

"No, just further over, you can see the Temple," Gatsby looked at Rose and she blushed.

Xing saw that his interest had strayed too long. A technique for gaining favour that he was familiar with. "You should go for a swim," he suggests, "cool down a bit."

"Not today, every other day, I swim across the Lake and back. Today, this heat, reminds me of being back in Afghanistan."

"Now there is another market we Chinese are doing well in."

Gatsby frowned so Xing let up.

"I have my eye on some more properties on the shore. I have a good list of interested Chinese clients. We can work together. You can furnish the houses with antiques," Xing couldn't help himself, "or do you just deal in reproductions and fakes?"

"Most of my things are genuine. But, you know, sometimes the reproductions are better quality than the real things," replied Gatsby. "Anyway your factories make the fakes."

"Only because we no longer have so many originals left after the Cultural Revolution."

"Maybe we should go back to the house, to get ready," I suggested.

"Let's go in style, it won't be long before summer is over," said Rose.

"Yes," said Becca, "lets take champagne and drink as we go down the motorway. It will be hilarious seeing people's faces."

Gatsby's face lit up at the idea, though not the practicality.

"Can we all get in your car?" I asked.

"Yes," replied Gatsby, "but its better to take two cars. I'll go with Xing and Rose. You and Becca go together."

"Okay," I agreed, much to Becca's disappointment.

"It'll be nice to have a chauffeur for the day," said Xing.

"No, I only hire him out for weddings and party nights, old sport."

"Only joking laoshi yundong," said Xing, "old sport," he explained.

"You'll be able to sit back, old boy," said Gatsby, "and enjoy the rest. You look like you could do with one."

"Yes, I've never been in a jalopy before, ha, ha."

Gatsby raised an eyebrow and looked at Rose. She smiled, embarrassed by Xing.

"You have a lot to learn about style old sport."

"It's an amazing car," I agreed.

"How about if Rose, Xing and I go in my boat to get the Beauford," said Gatsby, "and Dan and Becca can go in Becca's car?"

"And we can come back in Becca's car when we all get back at Gatsby's tonight," said Xing.

"Great," said Becca, unconvinced but resigned. Rose nodded.

As we got ready in the house Xing went up to get a white fedora. He came to the driveway and stood, waiting for approval. "Very dapper," said Rose.

"You'll need a hat that stays on if we drive with the top down," said Gatsby.

"Didn't realise it went fast enough," Xing replied, "anyway, it has a string to go in my button hole."

We shadowed Gatsby's car all the way to Manchester. Sure enough Xing's hat kept coming off until they put the roof up. Then Becca insisted on playing cat and mouse, on the motorway, overtaking and undertaking. Just to keep her stimulated on the journey. She was addicted to thrills and it didn't seem to matter how uncomfortable it made me feel. It was also then that I began to realise how she had a propensity to talk incessantly, about nothing. I value conversation most when people speak seldom but are eloquent, whereas she just babbled like a brook. So it was with great relief that we arrived in China Town, past the Dragon Gate. The cameras turned to look at us as we parked outside the Casino.

"Come on," rallied Xing. Then inside he announced, in a loud voice, "Becca is going to play some Mah Jong for us."

"It's too hot to play. And I've been drinking," she replied in a loud voice, then whispered to me, "I'll lose deliberately. They'll be back and then I'll play again and clean them out."

And after three middle aged men assembled at the Mah Jong table they started to play. I recognised Meihua at a blackjack table. She stopped dealing and headed over to us. Gatsby looked at Rose. Her jealousy was clear.

"Ni hao Dan," said Meihua.

"Ni hao Meihua," I replied.

"How do you know her?" asked Becca, pausing her game.

"We met at Gatsby's," I replied.

"Well stay away from her, she's dangerous. Her husband works in the kitchen here. Poor guy, its surprising he hasn't turned her to Chop Suey."

"Ni hao Xing," said Meihua.

"I think you should get back to your table," said Xing.

Meihua whispered something in Xing's ear and nodded over to the kitchens. Then she stood with her finger tips on Xing's shoulder so that Rose could see. Xing brushed them off as Rose turned and headed for the powder room. And for the first time I saw uncertainty and panic mixed with the usual anger in Xing's eyes.

Becca was listening and passed it on to me. "From what I can tell, she says that someone has told her husband what's going on and that she's going to leave him tonight. She's going to go to the apartment. And that she's going to tell Rose and everyone about their relationship on Facebook and Weibo if he won't." I was a bit stunned. I puffed my cheeks and blew from my mouth.

"I detest that woman," Becca continued. "Her husband Jian Ji is such an honest, hardworking man. He's got a bit of a temper, but he deserved to know."

Meihua's husband came to the kitchen door and was watching, furious. He came into the room and started ranting at Xing. Then pushed him over the Mah Jong table, sending the tiles everywhere. Two men came over and led him back to the kitchen. The other players looked angry. They were winning and the game was ruined.

"Sorry gentlemen," said Xing as he bowed. "Please have a drink on the house." Then he turned to us. "Okay, its time to go. We need to get to your warehouse. Becca, go get Rose."

"We only just arrived," said Gatsby. "I was wondering what else might happen here."

"We were only popping in for one game," replied Xing, flustered. "And now that's been cancelled."

"Let's walk," I suggested, "it's the Northern Quarter, isn't it."

As we gathered back to leave Rose asked, "Who was that woman. You seem to work a lot with her. What did she want?"

"She's a nobody. Don't worry I'll sort this all out," replied Xing. He then spoke to the receptionist and the two men came out to see him. He took them to a corner and gave them a key. I could see them put gloves on and head back to the kitchen. I still had my eyes to the kitchen door. And as we all descended the stairs. I saw them return, carrying something in a plastic bag.

We headed through the streets to Gatsby's vast warehouse. It was blissfully cool in the building. And inside Gatsby threw the lights on and we started to look at the furniture, records, clothes, shoes, bags, ornaments, clocks, statues, books…

"See, these clocks, they would make great presents to export to China," I said.

Rose laughed. "They are a symbol of death in China."

"Don't worry Dan, there's plenty here, I'm sure you'll find something," said Gatsby.

Rose and Becca honed in on the clothes rails. They went to search through the various hats and jackets, looking in dusty old mirrors. Then tried various luxurious but dusty furs

"I'm just going to have a look around," said Xing as he wandered into the warehouse.

"Whatever," said Rose, frostily. She looked around and then walked quickly over to a Chinese Calligraphy set. Gatsby followed. "It's a white Jade brushpot, Qing Dynasty, 18th Century. See the scholars in the landscape. And here's a blue and white 'fish pond' brush washer, mark of Xuande period." She nodded in thanks at his explanation. "You know he's not been completely faithful," continued Gatsby.

But Rose was too in love, or her pride was too hurt to accept that there was no excuse for Xing's actions, saying "Oh, he's always been faithful."

Becca just went along with it and expected me to do the same. It seemed like she expected me to understand, that Rose and Xing were our "meal ticket" and that she would drop me if I didn't go along with her. I didn't want to be there, only Gatsby had any genuineness left. I had lost mine.

Gatsby backed away and put on some old records and Becca encouraged us all to dance a bit of the Charleston, just for a laugh. So we danced, to stop her pestering us.

Xing returned and stood staring at the fancy dress spectacle. "I just don't get it. Why invest in Vintage when people can go to the high street and get clothes at a fraction of the cost?"

"Because they are made in sweatshops," replied Gatsby, "and have no quality."

"But we can reproduce all things Vintage."

"Yes, without the heart, without the heritage, just for money."

"Pah, what heritage. History is all just a fabrication anyway, 100 years ago all your 'Vintage' was made in sweatshops in this country or out somewhere in the British Empire. You know your Vintage is like your history. You mix a couple of original items, or facts, with cheap copies, or lies, and are then happy with the final lie to yourself that you dress well and have a great country."

"And you're just one hundred percent superficial, all surface appearances. No substance and quality to you," said Gatsby.

"I'm superficial," replied Xing. "You're the one who adopts a fantasy identity. Pretending you're someone that you're not." Xing gestured with his head, pointing around. "Most of the stuff here is just second hand junk People pretend that it's good because they can't afford better." He looked at Becca who was swanking in a fur stole. "Young people wearing their grandma's clothes. You have an English phrase 'mutton dressed as lamb', well this is 'lamb dressed as mutton'."

"Are you just here to criticise. Like I said, I want to export to China. Either you want to work together or you don't."

"You can work for me," replied Xing. "I want to send my containers back to China full of your good antiques. But none of your rubbish."

"No deal. I work for myself. I'm my own man. I'm prepared to work as a partner with you, or not at all."

"Yes, but you need my contacts, my Guanxi."

Gatsby knew that Xing was right. Everything that he now wanted was connected with Xing.

"Your MBA from Harvard is just a piece of paper, an expensive picture to frame and hang on your wall. Like one of these paintings, only it doesn't get any more value the older it gets. Enjoy looking at it, but it won't do you any good without my contacts."

Gatsby realised that Xing wanted to defeat him completely. "There's something for everyone here," said Gatsby, throwing his arms wide open. "Look, Mah Jong sets for Becca, easels for Dan, vanity units for Rose. And Xing..." he picked up a toy car... "yes, contacts to get you out of all kinds of accidents." He slammed the car onto the table.

Rose glowered and Becca hid a smile. I fumbled with a typewriter that had caught my eye.

"Below the belt, laoshi yundong," laughed Xing. "Lets face it, you have to work for me, if I want you that is."

"No chance. Not for all the tea in China, old sport."

"You over-estimate your value. And whilst we're at it, I don't want you pestering Rose any more."

"I really don't know why you moved across from us," said Rose, putting down the fur and moving to Xing's side.

Gatsby backed away. "I've been there for years."

"I don't want you to communicate with her in any way. Not by phone, text, Facebook, e-mail, anything. Or I'll get the police and have you arrested for harassment. For stalking."

Gatsby was shocked. He turned to Rose and she turned away.

"I've not done anything of the sort. I've been as embarrassed to see her as she was to see me. I was just trying to be friendly again. To put everything right."

"Yeah, and then you got carried away. Look, once upon a time, you danced together. But she never loved you. You were never her type. And you still aren't. Just accept it, or are you too in love with yourself to believe it."

"I'm sorry, really, really sorry. I mean I know I model myself on the Great Gatsby, but not on everything he does. I guess you did fit the picture, in that I loved you once, but I moved on long ago. Then when I saw you again a flame came back, but you clearly think I'm more in love with you than I am. And I never tried to impose myself on you. It was just if you felt something then maybe we could, I mean I know Xing was having affairs." Rose slapped him in the face and Gatsby reeled back into an old chair and started to break down.

"I only ever loved one person, and to know that they don't love you. How can you have not loved me when we connected together so well. When you made me so happy and everything felt like it was right when we were together. How could you not have felt like there was something there. All the things that I have are nothing compared to how I felt for you."

"We did get along," replied Rose, "and we danced beautifully but there was nothing there. No chemistry. It's Xing I love, and I forgive him the things he does. I can't help it. Just like you can't help loving me. The way he is doesn't mean I might start loving you, it just means I hurt more and more, until I cry myself to sleep. But I know that he still loves me because he loves our son and if all Xing's love for me comes to me through our son then that's enough to keep me going."

Xing raised an eyebrow. "I do love you. But if you want to be like that then maybe we should split up." Becca could see his bluff.

"No, no, please," cried Rose, "see what you've done," she spat at Gatsby.

"And you, Gatsby," said Xing, "stop feeling sorry for yourself. All this is just a front, a show, to hide the real you. Only you need to hide from yourself as much as hide from other people. Look at the lives you've ruined with your stuff," he looked at Becca. "Just because you're screwed up you don't care if you screw everyone else up. I won't have some crazed drugs dealer trying after my wife." Xing was stabbing his fingers at Gatsby.

"I don't deal drugs, old sport. I just tolerate them at my parties. If I didn't turn a blind eye then half of my 'guests'," he stared at Xing, "wouldn't come."

Xing grabbed the sobbing Rose. "Come on, we're going. Lets get a taxi."

"All the way back to Windermere?" asked Becca.

"Yes, we've had enough here."

"I'll drive you," said Becca.

"Thank you," said Rose.

"Yes, thank you," added Xing, "though if you want to keep your job I don't want you at any more of his parties."

"Are you coming Dan?" asked Becca.

"No, I'll stay here."

"Suit yourself," she replied.

"And I don't want you swimming anywhere near our house," shouted Xing as he left the warehouse.

When they'd gone Gatsby said he wanted to be alone. But I didn't believe him. He had no one. I had to go back with him. I owed it to him.

It was sputtering, not raining as we left China Town in the Beauford. When we passed near the Hilton there was a big crowd and a police cordon. We stopped in the warm night and asked what had happened.

"A jumper," said one bystander.

"Murdered his wife in an apartment in the tower," continued another. "Both worked at a casino in China Town. And she was a prostitute. Called Jian something."

"Meihua?" I asked from the car.

"Yeah, something like that. He stabbed her in the heart. Then jumped."

I got out and pushed my way through the crowd. It was all just a bloody mess. The body cleared away, covered over. I felt sick. Not just the kind of retching that you get from a repugnant sight, but a deep down disgust at the whole situation, my life and the fact I was connected to all of this. It was all beyond the pale.

On the motorway back we pieced together the scenario. I thought that I was being paranoid but Gatsby was completely serious. Gatsby's conclusion was surreal, like out of some bizarre gangster movie.

"Meihua was found dead, her husband, the cook Jian Ji, was blamed. Meihua took the lift to the apartment above the Hilton. Two of Xing's men then killed her with one of Jian Ji's knives that they had taken from the kitchen at the casino. Then they told him where she was and gave him a key to the apartment. Told him that he should go to see her or one of them took him up there. Either way he went up and he found her with a knife in her heart. Then they threw him from the window."

"You're mad," I told him, "a complete fantasist." And yet I was being swept along. I believed him.

"The problem is, the police will know it's Xing's apartment. It will be registered in Meihua's name or Xing's."

"Why's that a problem?" I asked.

"Because he'll still be kept out of the courts and the papers. Guanxi."

When we were back in the lakes the water pounded the roads, splashing in small lakes that stretched along the tar. We resolved that we would see Xing, to sort it out. Gatsby hardly talked as we drove the final way to reach Xing and Rose's mansion. He stared intently as we navigated the narrow roads, his caution overwhelmed by his anger. He rang the intercom and we entered the grounds, past the dragon dog statues. Gatsby banged on the door.

Xing opened and Gatsby fired his accusation. "You arranged for those poor people, for Meihua and Ji, to be murdered."

"I don't know what you are talking about."

"Well the police, MI5, the embassies, the papers, everyone should know about it," insisted Gatsby. "Unless we can come to an arrangement."

"I have no idea what you are talking about. But just out of interest, what kind of arrangement?" asked Xing.

"This house, old sport."

I backed away, shaking my hands. "Nothing to do with me." I turned and walked away, shaking my head. Out a side door and into the rain and darkness.

Chapter 8

GATSBY PICKED ME up on the wet road from Xing and Rose's. I was grateful for the lift but not the company. It seemed so clear to me what a mercenary he was. I didn't want to speak to him, yet I wanted to know who he really was. How he had really become so rich.

"Jim, I don't understand you. You hide behind a fiction and yet you've made so much money. It doesn't add up. Where did it all come from? Are you some kind of gangster, or into future trading or insider trading? Is that what your business calls are?"

"My business is my business. I'm still evolving Dan," said Gatsby

"No, you keep changing identities." I replied, "But that's not evolving, it's just changing, dodging anything real. You're a walking anachronism. Only you're not even living in the past. You're just living in a movie from the past. And stalking Rose."

"I guess I just got carried away with the fantasy of being Gatsby. But I didn't move because I was stalking Rose or acting out a movie. It's true that it's like I'm living in a movie, but it just feels better when I do. It was a more elegant age." He paused. "I don't really believe in what I'm doing and it has no real meaning. But the reality of it is that we've lost the war and the only things left with any meaning are the simple pleasures. Family, warmth, health, nature, walking, swimming. I could give up all my money tomorrow just for those. But what's the point of that? I keep it to try and stop people destroying everything left in this country."

"What by selling all our antiques abroad."

"I'll keep the best things here when I can."

As far as I was concerned he was a hypocrite, an opportunist and a liar. I wanted no more to do with him. We drove in silence. Yet when we pulled up at his gate, as I was about to get out, he put his hand on my shoulder. "Dan, you're a good egg."

I brushed it off. "Whatever."

I was afraid, constantly thinking that Gatsby must be mad to blackmail Xing over a murder. I thought that I should go to the police, but I had no evidence, and I would be next on the hit list. I thought that perhaps I should tell Xing that I was no informer.

I had had enough. I began to pack my things. I didn't want to be anywhere near to these people any more. I didn't want to owe them or be obligated in any way. But I was tied up with them. There seemed to be only one way out. So I went over to Gatsby's to persuade him that we should go to the police.

He wouldn't have it and wouldn't say why. Said that I would understand more if he told me about his background. His pains and struggles to get anywhere in life.

"I've always been a perfectionist and the war reinforced it, it told me that perfection was the only antidote to horror. Horrors that stay with me."

"Even if you get perfection," I replied, "it never lasts."

"No, I once thought Rose was perfect, even her short temper. But I once mistook perfection for love. Funny how a love that feels eternal can fade. The eternity only ever lasted in a moment, tricked us, sorry, tricked me, into an illusion. You see, love is a lie, but perfection, that can be true. Love tells you it can last, perfection is happy to be eternally in that single, fleeting moment."

"Which perfection, whose perfection?" I asked.

"Whatever any of us can find." He stared blankly. "The likes of you, Dan old chap," he paused, "have no idea what living is. Living is being consumed with fear that you might die at any moment, yet still grabbing presence of mind to overcome that fear. That's why I long for perfection. Coz it is the only thing as intense as fear. The only thing that overcomes fear. That's why Muslim kids were blowing themselves up in Afghanistan. Because they'd been promised perfection in the afterlife, in a life away from all the pain and squalor that we'd been making for them. That's why all of us, sometimes, need to lie about having something perfect to look forward to, just so we can make it through."

"I don't see how any of this helps," I leaned forward. "What about getting the police?"

"Dan, the world is a mess. It's corrupt. The best thing you can do is not get involved. He'll kill you."

"And what about Rose, we can't just leave her with him."

"It's her choice old sport. When I said I was going to Afghanistan she got another boyfriend. We danced and she waited for me to kiss her. I wouldn't because she had a boyfriend already. I was waiting for her relationship to end. But she didn't end it for me. I was mad at her. Called her all sorts of things and vowed never to dance with her again. I couldn't understand it. I would wake up with a start and say out loud, "she doesn't love me!" I thought that maybe she had been waiting and that if only I'd had the courage to tell her I loved her, then she'd have told me she loved me too. But I left it too late. So I tried the other night, pretended to her, to myself, that I was just making amends. But I tried, just in case there was some spark left. I tried even though I'd already lost her as my ideal."

"You know in Afghanistan," he continued, "I'd see girls and women, with hair covered, that would remind me of Rose. Like she had come over to be there, for some inexplicable reason. I'd want to go up and take scarves off to check. I'd created some impossible hope. I'd see pictures in magazines and think they were her. Then, when my mates started being blown apart I started waking up with nightmares about them and it replaced my nightmare that Rose didn't love me. That she had left me with no dream, no perfection. She's nothing to me now."

"Yes, but she's still a person and we should get her to leave the house with her son. To get them away from Xing. You made a mistake before, by not telling her you loved her. Now you have to ask her to leave Xing, for the sake of her son. To get them away from that psycho."

"It's too late. She has to find out about him for herself."

"Please. I'll ring up and get her to the phone, then put you on. She'll listen to you because she knows you know about these things. You live in that world."

Gatsby looked quizzical.

"You know, gangland dealings."

"I don't know what you think of me," replied Gatsby. "Besides, if we got Rose out it'll just be a life of hiding for her. Of being afraid of her shadow, of the tentacles of Xing. I don't mind facing the danger. I had it every day in Afghanistan, walking down the road where a bag of rubbish, or a tin can could be a bomb that will blow your legs off. I don't mind coz the screams of my friends echo and tell me to get revenge over your enemy because justice won't let it be otherwise."

As we talked we wandered to the lounge, where he stood on a chair and got a box down from about a cabinet. Inside was a hunting shotgun. Gatsby cleaned it with a wire brush from a box and filled a pouch of cartridges.

"So that's why I made this perfection," he pointed around him, "grasping at history, at the past, at some former glory. Trying to make the illusion that there is something grand, something worth believing in. And that's why Xing isn't interested. The Chinese Communists destroyed their history in the Cultural Revolution and are now trying to find themselves again. But this is our past, our perfection, our dream. And the Platonic ideals, the real moments of perfection just slip further and further away from us. But I won't let Xing have all this. I'm going to have my perfect twist."

"Yes, yes," I said, not really listening. I had only one thing on my mind. "So, please ring Rose in the morning. Tell her about it, tell her that it'll all be on CCTV. They watch everything these days. Like God."

"Alright old sport."

"Promise?"

"Yes. But it'll turn out that the CCTV at the Hilton 'wasn't working properly.' So I'm doing this my way. You better get some sleep. I've got some calls to make. Some arrangements to make with some friends of mine."

I decided not to stay at Gatsby's. I didn't want to be caught up in some kind of gangland battle. It was safer to be in the lodge. Back there I had a text from Becca. She was at Xing and Rose's. Told me that she wanted to know what all the fuss was about. I knew she was too embedded in Xing's empire to trust. I sent a reply. 'Not feeling 2 good, will txt 2morrow xxx.'

I finished packing my cases, my easel, and paints. Last of all I shoved the box of table croquet into a plastic bag, though I wasn't sure that I really wanted the memento. I was determined to go back to London, to stay with my parents in Golders Green for a while, until everything blew over. I just wanted things to be back the way they were. After I'd packed I slumped into my arm chair, determined not to sleep. I sat listening to the hooting of an owl in the woods. The supposedly wise bird, associated with Athena, Goddess of Wisdom, was really just a hunter. But by the time I began to imagine its nocturnal prey I had fallen asleep.

That night in Chinatown the friends of Jian Ji and Meihua were mourning and the staff at the Casino were stunned. But there was no one to really look out for the couple. The police searched within the community for some contact details. Meihua's sister was the only family in England. All other family was in China. Their apartment was empty, except for the police and Yingli. She was too distraught to say anything. Finally they got a Chinese lady as interpreter.

Yingli insisted that her sister wasn't a prostitute. Said she had no idea what happened. Said she had never been to the Tower. Didn't want to be sent to prison or back to China. A heavy hand had been placed on her by Xing's men from the Casino. They knew she wouldn't talk about Xing and that she was too naïve to think that anyone but Jian Ji could've killed Meihua. Everyone knew he had a temper. Only Meihua's rivalled it. Xing's men had control of her, they had already planned out her destiny. Drugs and prostitution. She wouldn't get far if she tried to run away. They would find her. And she knew that her family back in China would pay the deadly price if she informed.

Wang Yingli cried for her sister. She cried for herself. And she cried for the fate of all the girls whose beauty and innocence had been smashed by men like these.

It was just after 9am when the morning light finally woke me. An envelope was through the door, with Gatsby headed invitation paper. 'Dan, old sport,' it read, 'you seemed annoyed with me. I've been trying to work it out. The only thing I can imagine is that you think my proposition to Xing is for my own financial gain. Please don't get me wrong. It's the only way to get some kind of justice and compensation to the families that have suffered. Your very good friend, Jim Baxter.'

I went over to see him, to make sure that he had phoned Rose. But he was gone. And his Beauford was gone from the garage.
I tried phoning him but there was no answer. I couldn't wait and left for London.

Later that day, as I unloaded my possessions at my parents' home in Golders Green, I got a call, from the police, that Gatsby's car was found abandoned by the Lake side with a towel and clothes on the seat. They asked me if I knew where Gatsby was, said that he wasn't contactable. I told them I'd give them his mobile phone number. They replied that his mobile was found in the car. That they were going through the numbers. They wanted to know if the car had been stolen. Hoping that Gatsby might not be 'lost' in the lake.

Chapter 9

THE WEEKEND PAPERS wrote of the 'murder and suicide' in Manchester and the 'disappearance' of Gatsby. His car was found parked by the Lake Windermere. His clothes on the back seat, with a towel and his mobile.

In the inquest of Jian Ji and Meihua only a few witnesses had seen the Chef arguing with Xing. The Mah Jong players and half the people in the casino could have given evidence. I can only suspect that they'd been pressured not to. But before the investigation got to a courtroom a renowned lawyer had all mention of Xing removed, on three technicalities: the credibility of the witnesses was questioned, it was claimed that insufficient notice was given of the evidence, and that the evidence had not been submitted in proper time. And so the hearing found, predictably, a verdict of murder and suicide.

It was weeks later that Jim's body was found by divers in the lake. He was found tangled in plants in his vintage swimming costume. His lungs full of lake water. Death by misadventure was recorded. Funny how such a strong swimmer could get caught out mid-lake. It must've been cramp or heart failure.

He had no close relatives and I was called back up to the Lake District to identify the body. The drawer was opened and his ashen corpse pulled out. It bore no relation to him. A decaying mass with physical resemblances; like the shape of the head and the length of the body. Without the clothes and carefully arranged hair there was nothing hinting at the person beyond the dead matter. Even if his beauty had been perfectly preserved, even clothed in his best suits, I wouldn't have seen what truly defined him.

The papers told of "The Modern Gatsby" and scrutinised his life. They drew parallels with the Great Gatsby in all but the manner of his death and loves. He was described as a charming but suspicious and shady figure. He was linked with antiques, society parties and drugs. One by one the press would describe and pick off former guests. Their names ruined. It was like a game of dominoes. To have been a regular at his parties became a badge of shame. And yet, as one who went to the parties, it was clear that the shaming was extremely selective.

Jim's distant relatives had nothing to do with him in life, but had inherited his property and, apparently, his many debts. The family sent just one of their sons to the cremation as a representative. A token gesture to ensure that the will was followed. It was the middle of a media storm so people shunned his ceremony. The small room was half full but, apart from Dwayne and the Johnson-Smythes, I could only guess who the people were. Old army friends, people that he'd worked with in property, people that he'd made use of and left behind, but still loved him. I had expected to see some of his other new business acquaintances and his new friends. None attended.

His will stated how he wanted his ashes to be buried. I volunteered to carry out his wish. Without ceremony. I wore my full tweeds in respect. The Lake District seemed so mournful that autumn. The warm russets drowned by the grey rain. The leaves were falling and lay wet in clumps. His ashes were placed in an antique urn and, according to his wishes, were buried in his grounds, at the Temple at the end of the slate paved walkway. I had dug a hole under one of the slate flagstones the previous day. Today I placed the urn in the hole and filled around it with earth then mixed a small amount of concrete and reset the stone.

The lake was choppy and there were storm clouds in the sky. At the shore the wind rustled the trees, like a ghost moving through the greenery. Like Pan, running wild, like Dionysus having thrown off his mortal form. The wind blowing us all, sharing with us our breath of life. Reminding us that we exist in that moment.

Then the heavens opened and the rain bounced off the lake walkway. I waited for it to pass. And headed back over the slippery walkway with my bucket and trowel.

As I approached the house I was please to see the Johnson-Smythes. But dismayed as they were checking how well a couple of workmen were loading up the removal van with antiques from the house. The two old grandfather clocks from the lounge stood at the entrance porch, ready for loading. They chimed, now in unison.

Then my heart raced as Xing came from behind the van. He was telling the Johnson-Smythes what to do. I had to pass him to get out. I felt like dodging him, hiding in the trees until he had gone. But the image of Jim's body, fixed in my memory, filled me with anger. I strode out towards them. The Johnson-Smythes blushed and didn't acknowledge me.

"Ni hao laoshi yundong," smiled Xing. "Have you forgotten your friends. Becca wants you to call."

I walked past, staring dead ahead. Xing was a mere ripple on the water. I didn't want anything to do with him, with any of them. I never called Becca. I hadn't texted her. I never wanted to give her the satisfaction of winning her game, of telling me that she wasn't interested in me any more. I was tired of being her convenient interest. Lasting love cannot occur in their kind of world. But where can it occur? All I knew was that I had to leave corruption, completely. I felt lost.

At the gate the old CCTV cameras were being dismantled by the CCTV installation men. In their van were the monitors that Jim used for watching over his antiques. I thought how they must have recorded evidence of Xing's men coming to get him. So I wound down my car window to speak with the men, then, on the side of the van I saw 'BTV Security', the firm owned by Xing's friend. I retreated to the car park and had to cling to a rhododendron bush as a yellow digger trundled past. It made its way to the field behind the car park where more lodges were being constructed, ruining the landscape. I got into my car and drove off.

That night I came back. I wanted to stand on the walkway, on the spot where Jim's ashes resided. I needed him to help me. I was lost. The gate to the mansion was open. So I headed past the house and down through the grounds. I used my mobile to light my way along the path through the woods.

The sky had cleared and the moon was strong in the blue of an early autumn night. The stars appeared faint, but were there.

The bright moon reflected on the water, sparkling, almost like the sun. It gleamed its cold light on the stones of the temple. A place where moss and vines had grown into the mortar, cracking it apart, dislodging stones. Something small and living that heaved apart the immovable. The walkway stood out, white against the dark water. And the tower sent black ripples out into the night lake.

The noise of modern music crossed the water. I didn't let it drown the sound of water lapping against the walkway. The cold moon hovered on the water, disturbed by the warm lights of the party at Xing and Rose's, which reflected like a search light. I turned from the silhouette of their three trees to look at the orange glow over Bowness and Windermere. Then a rapper announced something indistinguishable in an angry voice. His roaring mixed with the roars and applause of the guests, breaking any chance of the harmony that I'd been trying to find.

On my way back through the woods I thought that I could hear voices in the sound of the water, that it was 'Gatsby' coming in from a swim, in the waves breaking on the shore.

But I finally accepted that he was gone. An owl hooted and I came to the lawns.

The house was dark. Just some faint lights left on in the rooms that helped me to discern its outline against the sky. I wandered up, across the overgrown lawns. At the edges of the terrace, statues of boys holding urns that I had never paid much attention to now seemed comforting. The gravel crunched underfoot as I passed the Greek urns with their small topiary trees and out around the front. I headed down to the gate.

A taxi pulled up. "Thanks a lot" said a girl as she got out and then headed up to the lodges. Life was going on, as normal, washing away the past. Re-growing over the ruins of history. Then I realised, what was left to do was to write this story.

I didn't want to paint a homage to him. His house, his car, all missed the point. And I couldn't bear to go back to the house and capture all its decay. I had left that behind.

So dear reader, I write his story. I only wish that he was still here to read it. For my own part, I won't have anything to do with Xing, Rose or any of that family or their money. I went back to leafy Oxford to renew my studies. To start again. To study for a Masters in Creative Writing. Just to wear tweed and ride an old vintage bicycle around Oxford and pretend that I remember better days.

This is my way of confession, my way to write the truth. I let you be the judge of whether I am vindicated, acquitted, absolved. You are my judge and priest. And if you choose to, then you go to the police with all this evidence.

Some Other Books By
A.D.PADGETT
(M.A., P.G.C.E., B.A.)

TALES FROM THE OLD COFFEE HOUSE
ISBN 978-0-9561587-8-9
23 tales from 23 regions of coffee production. Each story designed to be read in the time it takes to drink a cup of coffee. Each story with a surprising flavour. Set off from the Old Coffee House on a journey around the world.

MURDER AT THE MIDLAND HOTEL
Murder on the Dance Floor No.1
ISBN 978-0-9561587-5-8
The first novella in a series of Murder on the Dance Floor mysteries. Rachel Foxe is called to investigate a missing husband and finds a deadly web of intrigue and deceit in a Charleston and Lindy Hop dance at Morecambe's famous Art Deco Midland Hotel.

SALSA MOST FOUL
Murder on the Dance Floor No.2
ISBN 978-0-9561587-6-5
The second novella in a series of Murder on the Dance Floor mysteries. Rachel Foxe is on a Salsa Dance holiday in Havana, Cuba, when a young dancer is found, ritually murdered, exposing the dark heart of the Salsa Dance craze.

THE RAINBOW SWASTIKA CONSPIRACY
ISBN 978-0-9561587-0-3
A 21st century world leader is arising against a background of dwindling energy resources, global warming, religious extremism, financial meltdown and the growing economic power of China, India and Saudi Arabia. David Wolfe, a Jewish sculptor, is caught up in Jewish, Christian, Muslim, Hindu and Buddhist prophecies, about Messiahs and the end of the world. He embarks on a global journey around art galleries, archaeological digs, business headquarters and religious sites to uncover the Rainbow Swastika Conspiracy.

www.ingramcontent.com/pod-product-compliance
Lightning Source LLC
Chambersburg PA
CBHW030529260626
47157CB00005B/1938